P

St. Helens Libraries

Please return / renew this item by the last date shown.
Books may be renewed by phone and Internet.

Telephone - (01744) 676954 or 677822
Email - centrallibrary@sthelens.gov.uk
Online - sthelens.gov.uk/librarycatalogue
Twitter - twitter.com/STHLibraries
Facebook - facebook.com/STHLibraries

KU-545-088

G21 - - JAN 2017 E74 - - MAR 2023

K11 - - APR 2017

Q8 - - JAN 2017

Q14 - DEC 2018

M3 - - APR 2019

G18

D9 - - MAY 2023

DANGEROUS LOVE

Left broken-hearted after a disastrous romance, Melissa Harley is looking forward to her new nursing job on the Greek island of Theros. She is determined to devote her energies to her elderly patient, enjoy the exotic scenery, and avoid all future entanglements with men. But then she meets Adonis personified in Russell, whose charms are irresistible. Melissa soon discovers, however, that nothing on the island is what it seems; and as her suspicions grow about the nefarious activities of those around her, so do her fears for her safety . . .

PHYLLIS MALLETT

DANGEROUS LOVE

Complete and Unabridged

LINFORD
Leicester

First published in Great Britain in 1977

First Linford Edition
published 2017

A catalogue record for this book is available
from the British Library.

ISBN 978–1–4448–3127–6

Published by
F. A. Thorpe (Publishing)
Anstey, Leicestershire

Set by Words & Graphics Ltd.
Anstey, Leicestershire
Printed and bound in Great Britain by
T. J. International Ltd., Padstow, Cornwall

This book is printed on acid-free paper

1

Melissa Harley turned her face to the slight breeze, enjoying its friendly caress as she stood on the deck of the small coastal ship plying its busy trade between mainland Greece and the islands in the shimmering Ionian Sea. She leaned against the ship's rail to watch the steamer going through the process of docking at the little quay on the island of Theros, and found herself looking straight into the quizzical brown eyes of an extremely handsome man whose bold gaze was alive with friendly animation. He was a fellow passenger, and smiled as she took in his appearance. He was very tall, and had a powerful body that showed not an ounce of fat and proclaimed that whatever he did in life, it had given him an edge of fitness which was exhibited in his every movement.

An answering smile touched Melissa's lips, but she scotched it and turned away, frowning on any advance that might come from him. She turned to the rail and gazed down at the creaming wake of the steamer as she stifled her feelings. When she glanced surreptitiously in his direction again, she was shocked to find him standing within two feet of her, his smile widening as he noted her start of surprise.

'Excuse my boldness,' he said pleasantly. 'I just had to speak. You're English, aren't you? In fact I'll stick my neck out further, and make a guess that you're on your way to Villa Ambios to nurse Mrs Kemp.'

Melissa was shocked, and gasped, 'How on earth do you know that?'

'So you're Melissa Harvey!' His smile was overpowering, and the twinkle in his dark eyes was pleasant to see.

'You're absolutely right.' Melissa smiled as her mind slipped into the level of his friendly mood. 'Ah! I know — you've just visited the Oracle at

Delphi and some of it has rubbed off on you.'

He laughed. 'I like that! But it's nothing so miraculous. I'm acquainted with Andrea Kemp, the daughter of your future patient, and your arrival has been eagerly awaited by the Kemp family.'

Melissa looked into his dark gaze and her heart seemed to miss a beat. She watched him intently as he glanced around the ship. He was really attractive, and she wondered how many innocent hearts he had broken in his time. She looked at the flat planes of his face, the clear-cut lines of his cheeks and forehead, and saw determination in the solid build of his chin. His thick black hair was short and curly, hanging appealingly over his forehead. He looked up suddenly, almost catching her off guard, and his gaze sharpened as he took in her tall, slender figure, blonde hair and blue eyes. She saw pure admiration appear in his gaze.

His lips twisted into a slightly

crooked smile. 'I'm Russell Vinson. I'm spending the summer at an archaeological dig at the old monastery just behind Villa Ambios, so I've met the Kemps, and I expect we shall see a lot of each other during the next few months.'

'I'm here to care for Mrs Kemp.' Melissa did not want to get too friendly, for she had just escaped from a love affair that had gone disastrously wrong. 'I doubt I shall have much time to myself.'

'So your name must be Florence Nightingale, not Melissa Harvey after all!'

Melissa laughed and turned to see that the steamer was slowing, preparing to dock. Greek seamen began dashing hither and thither, some preparing to unload passenger luggage and others making ready to land deck cargo. Their voices rose cheerfully on the hot air of a perfect summer afternoon.

'Do you have transport arranged?' Russell enquired. 'I'm being picked up by Professor Allen, who's in charge of the dig. We could drop you at the villa.'

'Thank you, but I expect to be collected.' Melissa was aware of the cold note in her tone and tried to de-ice it. She smiled. 'It was nice meeting you, Russell.'

'Well, I wish you luck, Melissa.' His smile was friendly. 'It was a pleasure talking to you. I shall certainly look forward to seeing you again. Bye for now. I can see the professor on the quay.'

'Goodbye,' Melissa responded, and watched his tall figure move away to join the throng already gathering around the gangplank.

She felt a little less lonely, and some of the chill in her breast seemed to thaw as she gazed across the bay to the distant horizon, where mountains, misted by distance, reared up beyond a dark blue strait. Those mountains were in Albania, she knew, for she had brushed up on her geography before leaving London. They had left the

Greek mainland on their way north from the port of Parga, and before that she had flown into Athens from London. She dragged her thoughts back to the present and prepared to go ashore.

Passengers were already streaming down the gangplank, Russell Vinson among them. Melissa's heart lurched when he glanced over his shoulder, caught her eye, and waved a friendly, carefree hand. She responded instinctively, and pulled her hand down quickly when she realised what she was doing. She looked at the people waiting on the quay and wondered if someone had arrived from Villa Ambios to meet her. She had notified her employers of the estimated time of her arrival, and was looking forward to her first meeting with her patient.

She waited until most of the passengers had departed before following, and the quay was practically deserted as she walked behind the two seamen who were handling her luggage, aware of the growing excitement and anticipation rising in her breast.

The seamen left her, their smiles revealing sparkling teeth in brown faces. Melissa looked around expectantly. She saw Russell talking to a tall professor-type man just along the quay. He looked at her again, then pointed just ahead to where a tall lean man dressed in a white linen suit was standing beside an expensive-looking car. Russell and the professor entered a car and drove away. Melissa stifled a sigh, fighting off a tight feeling of encroaching loneliness.

'Nurse Harley?' The tall man in the white suit paused in front of her, his blue eyes shaded by the wide brim of his hat. His sharp features were pale, as if he did not enjoy the best of health. She judged his age to be around thirty years. His eyes, holding a piercing quality in their fathomless depths, seemed to bore right through her.

'Yes,' she acknowledged, slightly breathless with gathering excitement.

'I'm Christopher Kemp. You're here

to nurse my mother.' His tone was impersonal, and when he met her gaze his eyes moved away quickly, as if he did not want to make contact, and his initial glance had given him all the information he required about her. He signalled to a nearby workman as he asked: 'Is this all of your luggage?'

'It is.' Melissa was taken aback by his brusque manner.

'I'm here to drive you to the villa. Please come this way. Your luggage will arrive shortly.'

Melissa followed him along the quay, and when she glanced over her shoulder she saw her cases being picked up by a workman. Gazing ahead once more, she quickened her pace to keep up with Christopher Kemp, for he thrust his way through the sightseers with no consideration for anyone on the quay.

She got into the car while he supervised the loading of her luggage. Then he joined her and drove away quickly, his gaze on the road ahead. Eventually they left the little town and followed a coast road that edged around the bay.

'Is it always this hot?' Melissa queried, finding the silence becoming strained as the moments passed. She glanced at his face, taking in his lean features and sharp chin. He did not look at her, but leaned forward and took a tighter grip on the steering wheel.

'It will get even hotter in a month or so, and if you're not accustomed to the heat then you won't like it here.' His voice was harsh, and cut through Melissa like a knife. She caught her breath. 'The last nurse left us after a month,' he declared, laughing harshly. 'I didn't like her,' he added.

'I see!' She wondered at his manner, and the thought crossed her mind that the nurse might have found good reason for leaving so abruptly. She was aware that Mrs Kemp had been seriously ill and needed the services of a professional nurse. But she could not understand Christopher's manner,

9

because she had come a long way to help his mother.

'You look too young for the job.' He glanced at her, animosity showing in his gaze. 'My mother's life will be in your hands.'

'I'm fully qualified,' she responded.

'I've no doubt!' A flicker of a smile crossed his lips, but there was a jarring note in his tone. 'My father is paying a great deal for your services.'

'I believe my bureau to be the finest of its kind, although this is my first case with them. I was a ward sister in a general hospital in London until recently.'

'Why did you leave?' An edge to his voice grated against Melissa's good humour. She began to feel deflated as his manner had the effect she presumed he intended.

She ignored his question. Her past was no concern of his, and she had no wish to talk of the heartache she had experienced in the past weeks. She looked at the scenery. This part of the island was broad and mountainous, rutted with soil-rich valleys containing vineyards and orange groves. The brassy sun was hot; its glare dazzled her unaccustomed eyes. She lifted a hand to shield her gaze and he glanced at her again, his lips pinched and tight.

'You'll need to wear sunglasses,' he observed. 'If you're not careful you'll become ill yourself, and then you'll be of no use to my mother.'

Melissa sighed inaudibly. She looked ahead, noting that the road was following the contour of the bay, and averted her eyes from the dazzling sea. There were cliffs overlooking the shore, darkly wooded with pines. The sky was over-bright and impossible to watch for long because of its glare. Far below she saw gleaming white sand and tiny waves breaking gently on the shore. She hoped she would find an opportunity to spend some time swimming and sun-bathing.

They were travelling a road that curved like a giant horseshoe around the bay, and when Melissa glanced back she saw the little town and the harbour on the promontory, while ahead the wooded slopes angling out to sea formed the second confining arm of the bay. Here and there on the dark slopes were little clearings, and set in each one was a brightly painted chalet or villa. Right at the point of the headland, poised on high cliffs and looking as if it were in danger of slipping down into the sea, was a large villa that raised a dark red roof to the faultless sky. Stone terraces formed a colourful setting to the side view, and below them the graduated tops of pines cloaked all approaches.

'It's very beautiful!' Melissa observed, glancing sideways at Christopher.

'You might not think so after you've been here some time — if you stay,' he replied.

Some of her pleasure evaporated, but Melissa forced a smile as she decided to ignore his manner and extract every jot of pleasure from her surroundings. She had never seen anything so lovely before, and wondered what kind of life this strange young man had experienced to become so jaundiced about the beauty around him.

'Is that the Villa Ambios?' she asked, pointing ahead.

'It is — and you may wish you had never set eyes on it by the time you've settled in.' He laughed cynically. 'That's if you get the chance to settle in! There's been some opposition in the family against having another nurse for Mother.'

'And obviously you are one of those who voted against it,' Melissa retorted.

'Whatever gave you that impression?' A grudging smile tugged at his lips.

Melissa did not reply. The road had drifted away from the cliffs, and they passed under the trees and slowed for an entrance. Black iron gates were open, and they continued under a canopy of pines that were so closely planted it was almost impossible to peer between their trunks. The air was heavy in the shade, and broiling hot. Melissa tried to moisten her lips. She glanced at Christopher's face once more, and when he threw a quick glance at her she felt constrained to speak.

'Why don't you want a nurse to care for Mrs Kemp?'

'She'll get better without your help. She's well on the way to recovery now, and I don't like strangers around the villa.'

'In times of sickness one has to endure some measure of inconvenience.'

He laughed again as the car turned a sharp bend and the villa slid into view. Melissa caught her breath. Her blue eyes shone as she studied the scene unfolding scene. 'It's enchanting,' she observed.

The car halted on a piece of flat, gravelled ground overlooking a carpet of golden-topped pine trees covering the lower slope that swept down towards the sparkling sea.

'Yes, it takes my breath away,'

Christopher answered in a bored tone as he alighted from the car. He walked around to open her door. 'Make the most of your pleasure now, because it won't last. You'll soon become jaded, like the rest of us, and then you'll hate the sight of the place. Of course, you can always leave, but the rest of us have to endure it.'

'Are you trying to put me off?' Melissa challenged as she emerged from the car. She looked into his eyes and saw a glint in their expressionless depths. 'I've been engaged to take care of Mrs Kemp, and I shall stay as long as I'm needed.'

'You shouldn't say it so firmly. You may retract that statement before you've been here very long. Leave your cases in the car and come with me.'

'Yes, Master,' Melissa replied in an undertone.

He turned abruptly and walked to a flight of stone steps that led to the terrace. Melissa followed him, slightly depressed by his hostility. They walked to the front of the villa, which overlooked the sea, and she paused to take a long look at yet more breath-taking views, the crowded pines on the foreshore, and the scintillating sea, like a mill pond right out to the distant horizon.

She liked what she saw. Tall trees hemmed in the villa, with the promise of cool shade about them. She caught glimpses of small, colourful birds flashing around in the sunlight, and heard their incessant twittering. Moving to the low wall forming a boundary to the terrace, she looked out over the tops of the trees and studied the wide expanse of blue sea in the background. The distant horizon seemed remote and mysterious, with faraway mountains looking like low clouds, misty and indistinct behind the haze that shimmered far out.

'Come in out of the sun.' Christopher Kemp's voice jarred the peacefulness of the afternoon. 'We don't want you ill with sunstroke, or something equally lethal. You're here to nurse my mother, not incapacitate yourself with your foolishness.'

Melissa exhaled sharply, telling herself that she would not tolerate much more of his attitude; her illusions were crumbling under his insistent unfriendliness. She turned to accompany him, but he moved on before she could reach him and strode into the villa. Melissa paused at the door and had a last, lingering look over a slim shoulder. Then, taking a deep breath of the tangy air, she walked into the building.

Christopher was nowhere to be seen, and Melissa hesitated at the end of a long hall. There was a half-open door on the right and she heard voices within. She recognised Christopher's surly tone, and then heard another man's voice, deep and resonant.

'She's coming,' Christopher was saying. 'But at the moment she's more interested in the scenery than Mother's health. I hope she'll keep her mind on her duties when she does take them up.'

Melissa set her teeth into her bottom lip and suppressed a sigh.

Christopher appeared in the door- way, looking impatient. 'Come in, Nurse, if you're quite ready,' he commanded. 'My father is waiting to brief you on your duties, and he can't wait all day.'

Melissa entered the room and a short, thickset man of about sixty arose from a desk and came around it with outstretched hand, a smile of welcome on his fleshy face. His dark eyes were intent, and seemed over-bright.

'Nurse Harley,' he greeted her in a friendly tone. 'I'm pleased you've arrived safely. Did you have a good trip?'

'It was fine, thank you,' she said with a nod, feeling some of her tension fade away. Here was a much friendlier welcome! She cast a glance at Christo- pher and saw his lips twisting into a sardonic smile, but she ignored him and concentrated on her employer.

'Christopher, tell Eugenie to come

here,' Louis Kemp said. He waited until the door closed behind his son. 'Now, Nurse, I want to tell you exactly what the situation is regarding Mrs Kemp. You've been told nothing by your bureau, I expect.'

'Nothing at all, except that Mrs Kemp has been ill after a nervous breakdown.'

'I wish that was all.' He suppressed a sigh and pointed to a seat. Melissa sat down as he returned to his chair behind the desk. 'I must tell you here and now that since Mrs Kemp came out of hospital, there has been a division in my family. My son Christopher is against having his mother home with a nurse in attendance, and my daughter Andrea said it might be better if Mrs Kemp had a male nurse in case she has to be restrained. But I want my wife to have the best care, and I think a female nurse is the only way to handle her.'

Melissa moistened her lips. Now she knew why Christopher Kemp was so unfriendly — he was set against her presence and purpose. The knowledge made her feel easier, and she listened keenly to Louis Kemp's words.

'Lucinda had more than a nervous breakdown,' he said, his eyes narrowed. 'She was mentally unstable for months, and after treatment and considerable improvement her doctor suggested that I bring her home to convalesce. She has to be watched all the time, and the Greek maid we employ is finding her too much of a handful unaided. Perhaps you should have been informed of the exact nature of this case before being taken on, but a nurse is a nurse, and you should be capable of handling all types of cases.'

'Psychiatric patients do need a specially trained nurse. Is Mrs Kemp violent?'

'She's more suicidal than anything.' He leaned forward in his seat and fixed Melissa with an unblinking gaze. 'If she was violent then she would never have been permitted to leave the hospital. If she ever contemplates violence, then it is against her own person, and that's why it's such a strain keeping her under observation. However, let me say this. Give her a try, and if you find you can't handle her then I'll return you to England. On the other hand, I fear, deep down inside, that we're wasting our time. I don't think she'll improve.'

Melissa frowned. 'I expect I shall be able to cope,' she said confidently.

'Good. That's the spirit. I was hoping you would say that. You certainly look as if you could handle anything that might come up. And always remember that I'm on your side. If you encounter trouble from any member of my family, then report it to me and I'll step in. You are to be treated as a guest while you're here, and I've issued orders to that effect. But I know my son and daughter. Their feelings over the way their mother should be treated run deep. However, you should get along well with Andrea. She has her mother's interests at heart.'

There was a knock at the door, and

Louis Kemp called an invitation to enter. 'Nurse, this is Eugenie, the maid,' he said. 'Eugenie, Nurse Harley. You will be working under her instructions in future.'

Melissa glanced round and saw a short, heavily built woman who stared unabashedly at her and smiled a friendly welcome. Melissa smiled in return, thinking that here at least was a potential friend. The woman was attractive, with a large round face and heavy brows. Her brown eyes glinted with pleasure as Melissa arose at the introduction.

'Hello, Nurse.' The woman spoke in a husky, accented voice. 'I've been looking forward to your arrival. I hope you'll like it here.'

'I'm pleased to meet you, Eugenie,' Melissa responded. 'I've already fallen in love with the scenery.'

'I want you to take very good care of Nurse Harley, Eugenie,' Louis Kemp said. 'See to it that she has everything she might need. And keep a close eye on Christopher; let me know if he steps out of line or tries to interfere with Nurse Harley's duties. Will you show her to her room now?' He glanced at his wristwatch. 'I expect Mrs Kemp is having her sleep at this time, so you may show Nurse Harley around the villa.' He glanced at Melissa and smiled. 'I'm sure you like swimming and sunbathing, eh?'

'I do. But I'm here to care for a patient, and I usually find my duties are a full-time job.'

'Nurses are responsible, caring people,' he mused. 'But we are not going to work you too hard. Arrange with Eugenie to split up the time that has to be spent with Mrs Kemp. Eugenie, explain the routine the doctor suggests we follow.'

'Yes, Mr Kemp. If you'll come with me, Nurse, I'll show you round.' The woman turned to the door and Melissa followed.

'I shall always be in the background, Nurse,' Louis Kemp said as Eugenie opened the door. 'And I repeat, if you have any queries or problems then don't hesitate to come to me.'

'Thank you, Mr Kemp, but I'm sure I shall cope. You can rest assured that I'll do my utmost.'

'I'm certain you will,' he replied cordially.

Eugenie led Melissa along a passage and then up a wide flight of stairs to a corner bedroom. A tall window looked out over the cliffs and the bay, and Melissa gazed from it, eager to satisfy her curiosity. The blue sea stretched away to the distant horizon, sun-dappled and serene.

'You should be happy here,' Gina said. 'You won't find life so very hard with two of us taking care of Mrs Kemp. She's fairly easy to control once you've gained her confidence.'

'You've been looking after her alone, haven't you?'

'Yes, and it's been difficult, but I think she's beginning to show improvement. We have to keep her locked in her room; there are bars at the windows, and she has nothing which she might use to harm herself. Have you had other cases like this?'

Melissa shook her head. 'I was a ward sister in a hospital before I came here,' she replied.

'Well, don't worry about anything. I'm always around if you need me. You mustn't be upset if Mrs Kemp doesn't take to you at first. She has strange ways. The doctor doesn't see her anymore unless we send for him because she won't have him in her room. So, you see, there are difficulties. But we manage quite well. I'm hoping that in the not-too-distant future Mrs Kemp will get back to being her normal self. She was such a lovely woman. But it was a tragedy that turned her mind, and perhaps we are wasting our time trying to turn back the clock.'

'I hope not!' Melissa spoke firmly, and, as Eugenie nodded her approval, added: 'You speak very good English, and what a lovely name you have.'

'I learned English at college, and

have always worked with English people. I've been the maid here for eight years. At first the Kemps didn't live here permanently, but since Mrs Kemp became ill they've stayed here. My friends don't call me Eugenie; I don't really like it. Call me Gina.'

'And you must call me Melissa.'

'But that's a Greek name. Do you know what it means?'

'I haven't the faintest idea.'

'Honey bee!' Gina laughed merrily. 'And it suits you. Your hair's the colour of honey and you're very beautiful. Your face shows gentleness, but there are shadows in your eyes. What made you leave the hospital in England to come here?'

'I was mistaken about a personal relationship.' Melissa suppressed a sigh. 'So I really needed a change of scene, and your island looks like heaven.' She smiled tensely as she considered the bad days of the recent past, when her heartbreak had seemed too heavy to bear and it felt like life hadn't been worth living. But now she was filled with high hopes that this wonderful scenery would create enough of a change to make her forget the unhappiness of the past. In point of fact, it seemed to her that the ghosts in her mind were already beginning to fade.

'I'm sorry if the questions I ask are too personal,' Gina said lightly. 'It's a national failing, you know. We Greeks do not mean anything by it. We'd like everyone who comes here to be as happy as we are. Now I expect you'd like to freshen up. The bathroom is next door on the right. Mrs Kemp's room is next to you on the left. I'll take you in to meet her later this afternoon. She always takes two tablets after lunch and usually sleeps until five o'clock. Your luggage will be brought up by Nick Stephanos — he's the gardener, and my boyfriend. Very soon we are to be married, and then I'll leave Villa Ambios. I'll be very sad to do so, because I love working here.'

'Congratulations,' said Melissa. 'I

hope you'll be very happy, Gina.'

'Thank you; and I hope you, too, find happiness on the island.' Gina's dark eyes gleamed with pleasure and the ghost of a smile tugged at her lips. 'I make your age at about twenty-two?'

'Twenty-five,' Melissa replied. 'But I haven't come here to seek happiness.'

'I hope Mrs Kemp will take to you. That's half the battle! It would have been terrible if Christopher had got his way and they didn't employ another nurse. And Miss Andrea was all for a male nurse coming in.' Gina suppressed a shudder as she turned to the door. 'Let me show you the bathroom, then I'll get Nick to bring up your luggage. Later I'll introduce you to Mrs Kanera, the housekeeper. She'll be a great help to you when you begin your nursing duties.'

'Thank you. I'm sure I'll get on very well. I was pleased at having been selected for the position.' Melissa pictured Christopher Kemp's face as she spoke. He seemed to be the only blot on the page of her arrival, she thought; and smiling reflectively, she dismissed all notion of him. He didn't count! It was Mrs Kemp who needed nursing.

When Gina departed, Melissa went to the window and once more gazed out over the sea, shading her eyes with a hand to divert the glare of the powerful sun. She was here at last, and all the grey days were left behind in England. She had made a complete break with her past, and whatever lay in the future, she would have no regrets. She had thrown off her old attitudes as if they were outdated clothes, and was looking forward with a natural optimism that had been repressed during the past two months. She was standing on a threshold where life would begin anew, and with a far better outlook.

2

Melissa awaited her first meeting with Lucinda Kemp with great anticipation. Accustomed to hospital work, she knew she would find it strange taking care of a single patient without the usual strict routine that she had always followed. But it would be a challenge, and she was determined to do her best no matter what happened.

Gina returned at length, struggling with Melissa's cases. Her face wore a rueful expression when Melissa opened her bedroom door.

'What on earth — ?' Melissa began.

'Nick is busy in the garden,' Gina explained, 'and I want you settled in before you start your duties. Before we check on Mrs Kemp, I'll take you down to the private beach. I expect you'll spend most afternoons down there.'

'If I can find the time,' Melissa observed.

'I'll see that you do.' Gina's eyes gleamed when Melissa began opening her cases and transferring their contents to the spacious cupboards and wardrobes built into the room. Gina kept exclaiming at Melissa's dresses, holding them up against her own shorter, plump figure and shaking her head. Melissa couldn't help smiling at her cheerfulness and enthusiasm. When they had completed the task, Gina took hold of Melissa's hand and tugged her toward the door.

'I'm off duty until four-thirty,' Gina said, 'so I'll show you the way to the beach. It's through the trees and down the cliff path. You must be very careful if you come this way when darkness falls, because it could be dangerous.'

But first Gina showed Melissa around the villa, and she was impressed by what she saw. As they went out to the front terrace, Melissa inhaled a deep breath of the perfumed air and told herself that if she lived here for a hundred years, this scenery would never lose its freshness and startling clarity.

They descended a flight of stone steps at one end of the terrace and followed a path that meandered through tall trees towards the beach. The air was pleasantly cool in the shade, with slanting rays of golden light stabbing down through the dark foliage and turning the narrow spaces between the upright trunks into an exotic fairyland of brightness and shade. The smell of pines and the more pungent perfume of honeysuckle caught at her throat. Birds were busy and, startled by the two women, flew hither and thither through the shadows like streaks of coloured flame.

Melissa's heart thumped with unaccustomed emotion as they went on, and she was gripped by a sense of unreality. The path became steeper, as if it were in a hurry to reach the shore, and a carpet of pine needles was spongy underfoot, deadening the sounds of their movements. They reached a fork in the path and Gina paused to point along the diverging way.

'That leads to Gregory Lombard's chalet,' Gina said. 'He's a close friend of the Kemps, and leases the chalet from them. Mr Lombard is a writer of travel books. There are a lot of English people on the island, and they all gather at times at Mr Lombard's chalet — he acts as a spiritual leader. This summer a party of archaeologists from London are digging at the old monastery on the hill beyond the villa. They'll be up there until October. From my bedroom window I can see them working. They have a yacht in the bay where Professor Allen lives — he's in charge of the dig. Mr Kemp has given them permission to use the private beach because it saves them miles getting to and from the monastery.'

'It all sounds very exciting. I met one of the archaeologists on the boat coming from the mainland — Russell Vinson. He seems a very friendly type.

Is the public allowed to view the site? I've always been interested in that sort of thing.'

'Then you must get to know Russell.' Gina laughed. 'Don't you think he's the most handsome man you've ever met? He's the youngest of the archaeologists, and comes to the villa to see Andrea.'

'I haven't met Andrea yet. What's she like? I hope I'll get a friendlier welcome from her than I received from Christopher. Is he always so cynical and impatient?'

'Yes!' Gina's face was suddenly grave, and she clutched at Melissa's arm. 'Watch out for him,' she said tensely. 'He's a strange man, and I sometimes get the feeling that he may eventually go the way of his mother.'

Melissa frowned at her words. She looked into Gina's dark face to see if she was joking, and grimaced at the degree of seriousness showing in her eyes.

'I am very serious,' Gina said. 'I must admit that I'm a little bit afraid of

Christopher. He associates with some undesirable men on the island, and I have suspicions about the nature of their business.'

'Unsavoury or criminal?' Melissa asked. 'Doesn't he have a job?'

'He was employed in his father's business until they left England. He sometimes goes back to London to check on what's happening there. But he doesn't need to work. The Kemps are millionaires.'

'What kind of business are they in?'

'Importing and exporting, but I don't know what they trade in.'

Melissa shook her head as they continued along the path, scrambling a little on the steeper parts. They emerged at length from under the trees to descend a flight of wooden steps to a stretch of coarse blue grass that fringed the pale beach.

The sand was quite firm. Melissa paused and shaded her eyes against the glare that was reflected brilliantly from the sand and the sea. The bay was well sheltered by the two long projecting arms of the twin promontories enclosing it, and in the distance to the right was the dark smudge of the town nestling at the water's edge. The colours around Melissa were vivid, the greens and gold seemingly alive under the glaring blaze of the sun. She glanced up at the faultless sky and was compelled to close her eyes against its brilliance.

'Do you like what you see?' asked Gina.

'I can't find the words to describe it,' Melissa responded. 'When I left England it had been raining non-stop for almost a week, and the wind was really cold. It was supposed to be June!' She inhaled deeply as the hot breeze caressed her face, the pungent mixture of orange blossom, pines and sea almost too strong for her senses.

'Do you like to swim?' Gina asked.

'I do, especially in these wonderful conditions. I was a great swimmer at school, and won medals.' Melissa smiled as they walked toward the shoreline. She could see a small white yacht at anchor two hundred yards out, but there was no sign of life aboard.

'We should go back to the villa and collect your bathing suit. You mustn't waste a minute of your free time.'

'And I mustn't get impatient about that,' Melissa replied with a smile. 'I'm not here on holiday, and I think I should meet Mrs Kemp before thinking of going off duty. My services have been hired, and I won't get paid for lazing around on a beach, no matter how heavenly it is. Tomorrow will be soon enough to think about having some time to myself. But will I be allowed to use the beach? You did say it's private.'

'Certainly you can use it. Even I am permitted to come down here when I'm off duty. Can you swim underwater with goggles and flippers?'

'I've never tried it.'

'Then you must. You would enjoy it immensely. It's just like being a fish, only better. Christopher is always under water, and even Andrea does it. Russell

Vinson is an expert too, and I think he's the man to teach you.'

'I'm wary of men at the moment.' Melissa's eyes darkened. 'And Russell Vinson is too attractive to be treated lightly.'

'So you've had trouble recently with a man,' Gina surmised.

'No comment,' Melissa countered.

'You'll get used to seeing Russell around!' Gina laughed. 'He's a very pleasant fellow, although Christopher doesn't like him.'

'From what I've seen of Christopher, I'd be surprised if he likes anyone,' Melissa replied.

They walked along the shore at the water's edge, their feet leaving no impression on the firm white sand. Melissa glanced repeatedly at the trees covering the whole coastal area. Many different shades of green were marked by clumps of cypress, cedar and oak, with tall, sturdy pines bristling everywhere. To Melissa's appreciative gaze it was an enchanted place, and she was uplifted by the sight of nature in full bloom.

When they reached another path that led upward through a natural fault in the cliff, Gina sighed and led the way off the beach. They gained the brow of a tree-covered hill and walked back to the villa from a different direction. Ahead, high and remote on a stark hill, Melissa spotted the ruins of a monastery, and saw figures up there moving around.

'I'll show you the monastery another time,' Gina said. 'Unfortunately we don't have the time right now.'

They approached the villa from the rear and, skirting the building to reach the front door, they came upon a car standing beside the terrace. Gina uttered an imprecation in Greek, and Melissa glanced at her. 'Is something wrong?' she asked.

'That's Andrea's car. She must have heard that you'd arrived. She hadn't intended to come back to the villa today. But I think you will get along well with her. She wanted a nurse to come and live in.'

'I haven't come here to care for Andrea,' Melissa said firmly, 'so her attitude won't worry me in the least. I'm here as a nurse, Gina, not as a guest, and there is a difference.'

Gina's dark eyes glistened. 'I'm pleased to see that you'll fight for yourself, Melissa. They won't be able to dominate you.'

'I found Mr Kemp very pleasant, and I'm sure he'll see to it that my duties are made as uncomplicated as possible.'

They entered the villa's extensive gardens, and came upon a young man in a remote corner stretched out on a patch of grass in the sunlight. He was stripped to the waist, his bronzed body gleaming in the afternoon light as he lay on his back with his hands beneath his head. He was asleep, and Gina held up a warning finger to Melissa.

'This is Nick,' she whispered. 'He told me he was too busy to take your cases up to your room.'

She darted away to fetch a pail that was standing under a tap protruding from a nearby wall, grasped it and hurried to where Nick was lying. Then she upended the pail and sluiced a torrent of water over the sleeping figure. Nick started up with a yell, rudely awakened and galvanised into movement. As he sprang to his feet, Gina threw down the pail and fled for her life, and he took off after her, dripping water on the path and uttering mild threats.

Melissa smiled as she lost sight of them in the further reaches of the garden, and continued on her way. She looked around, recognising hibiscus among the exotic blooms filling the air with their heavy perfume, and wondered at the names of the flowers that she did not know. There were small thickets of summer jasmine here and there, creating a stunning effect.

When she approached a front corner of the villa, Melissa heard voices, and paused before turning the corner and revealing herself on the front terrace. A man and a woman were talking together. Melissa heard their words distinctly and, because they seemed to be talking about her, she paused to listen.

'Have you seen the new nurse yet?' demanded the man.

'No, Gregory. I've only just returned. I saw Christopher in town and he told me he'd met her at the boat. He said he'd given her a rough time, so I've come back to try and smooth things over. I want her to have a fair chance of nursing Mother.'

The woman's voice sounded mellow and soothing, and Melissa moistened her lips as she prepared to step into view. But in the back of her mind she wondered why Christopher Kemp would want to give her a rough time. Surely his mother's health was of paramount importance to him!

She moved around the corner and approached the couple standing on the terrace by the front door. The woman was tall and slender, dressed in a lightweight white skirt and a red blouse; her dark hair was shoulder-length and sleek. The man was also tall, but very thin, and his fair hair was thick at the nape of his neck. He heard Melissa's footsteps and turned his head quickly, his keen blue eyes narrowing to slits. He spoke to the woman in an urgent undertone, and she looked over her shoulder, but her face was practically obscured by the dark sunglasses she was wearing.

'Hello,' she greeted Melissa instantly, turning slowly and removing her glasses. Her teeth glinted in a bright smile of welcome. 'You must be Melissa Harley! I'm Andrea Kemp, and I'm so pleased you've arrived safely. This is Gregory Lombard, our neighbour.'

'Is that how you regard me, Andrea?' demanded Gregory in a mock-serious tone, but he was smiling at Melissa, and came forward to take her hand briefly. 'I'm pleased to meet you, Nurse. I hope you'll be happy here. This is a wonderful place.'

'Hello,' Melissa responded. She looked into Andrea's eyes, deciding that she was about thirty years of age, and a most attractive woman. 'I've been getting my bearings. Everything is too beautiful for words.'

'Have you met my mother yet?' Andrea enquired.

'Not yet. I believe she's asleep at this time.'

'You're very beautiful!' Gregory said gently. 'When I first heard that a nurse was coming, I imagined you'd be a battle-axe of a woman with a face like a lemon and a manner to match.'

'I think I have a few more years to go before that description will fit me,' Melissa replied lightly, and they laughed. She saw approval in Andrea's dark eyes and felt a spark of hope that here she might find friendship.

'Have you settled into your room?' Andrea asked. 'I ensured that it was well decorated and furnished.'

'It's a lovely room,' Melissa said,

nodding. 'I'm sure I'll be very comfort-able.'

'What are you first impressions of Theros?' Gregory asked. 'I think first impressions are most important, don't you? I wish I were in your shoes right now, arriving for the very first time. I'm afraid I've forgotten what my thoughts were when I first came, although most of my impressions are still quite vivid.'

'It's breath-taking,' Melissa responded. 'I expect it'll take me quite some time to grow accustomed to it.' She glanced across the tree tops towards the sea.

'That's how it affects everyone the first time they see it,' Andrea observed, 'and it'll never become commonplace. Every morning when I wake up, I look out across the bay and tell myself that I'm the luckiest person alive.'

'I feel as if I'm dreaming,' Melissa admitted. 'I hope I'll have the opportu-nity to look over the whole island while I'm here.'

'I hope I'll have the opportunity to

show you the sights,' Gregory said eagerly.

'Thank you.' Melissa smiled, looking at him more intently. He seemed youthful in appearance, and before she had crossed the terrace she imagined him to be in his thirties, though close up she could see lines and wrinkles on his face; his fair hair was grey at the temples.

'I hate to drag myself away,' Gregory continued in a rueful tone, 'but I have a business appointment that can't be postponed.' He took Melissa's hand again, smiling. He was handsome and charming, and there was a fixation in his expression that gave him an intriguing air. 'I shall look forward to seeing you again, Miss Harley.' He paused and his smile widened. 'As I'm not your patient, I refuse to regard you as a nurse. Perhaps I can visit you soon, when you're off duty? I should very much like to show you around the island — I'm an authority on it.'

'Gregory writes travel books,' Andrea said, 'and he's very much an authority on most places in the area. He's also a great charmer, Nurse, so be on your guard.'

Gregory smiled as he turned away. He walked to the stone steps at the end of the terrace before turning to look back at them. 'I'll show my face again this evening,' he said, and then departed, moving lightly down the steps and following a path through the trees.

'Can I help you settle in?' Andrea asked. 'All of this must be very strange to you, especially if you left a family in London.'

'I have no family. My parents are dead.'

'No other ties?' Andrea paused. 'Sorry, I don't mean to pry. But a lovely lady such as yourself must have many friends.'

'There's no one at the moment.' Melissa waited for a reaction in her breast and, when nothing happened, she sighed in relief: it was the first time since her romance had disintegrated that she did not feel a wayward tugging of dark emotion at the memory. She drew a deep breath and held it for a moment, smiling as tension seeped away. It seemed that Philip Granger had slipped down from his pedestal in her mind and had faded into obscurity.

'You must be dedicated to your career,' Andrea mused. 'You won't need to wear a uniform around the villa, will you?'

'I have uniforms with me, but it's up to Mr Kemp how I present myself.'

'If my father hasn't already mentioned it, then it must have slipped his mind. But we agreed before your arrival that you shouldn't wear a uniform. It might upset Mother.' Andrea paused. 'Do you know anything about the case?' she asked hesitantly.

'I didn't before I arrived, but Gina's given me some details.'

'So you've met Gina. You should get along quite well with her. She's been very good with my mother. I don't know what we'd have done without her. You'll have to rely on her a great deal at first. She's the only one who can handle Mother during her difficult times.'

'I'm sure we'll manage.'

'We'll have to go into the matter of your off-duty periods. I don't know what a nurse's normal working hours are, but you mustn't let us work you too hard or too long. When you're off duty Gina will stand in for you, and as we are quite some distance from the town we must arrange transport for you.'

'Thank you,' Melissa said with a nod. 'I'm sure I'll soon slip into a routine. After the first few days you'll barely notice my presence.'

'You've already met my brother Christopher!' Andrea's face became impassive. 'I saw him in town and he admitted giving you a rough time. I apologise on his behalf because he would never apologise for himself. Just put his attitude down to ignorance, and tell me if he gives you any problems. I'll soon put him in his place.'

'Hello there!' a voice exclaimed from the opposite front corner of the villa, and they both looked round quickly.

Melissa narrowed her eyes as she watched the figure striding towards them, and her heart seemed to miss a beat as she recognised the voice. It was Russell Vinson. She studied him critically as he came across the terrace with lithe strides, and caught her breath as she realised that since their meeting, he had remained in her mind.

'I see your new nurse has arrived,' he called.

'Hello, Russell,' greeted Andrea. 'Russell Vinson, Nurse Harley!'

'We met on the boat earlier.' Russell advanced with outstretched hand, a smile on his face. 'Hello, Florence!' His grip was firm and friendly. 'I'm pleased to meet you again. Glad to see you've arrived safely.'

'Hello again,' replied Melissa, a tingle of emotion trickling through her at their contact. She was keenly aware that he was disconcertingly handsome.

'Her name is Melissa, not Florence,' Andrea cut in.

'Is it really? You disappoint me. When I saw her on the boat I thought at once that she was a regular Florence Nightingale.' He smiled at Melissa. 'Are you interested in archaeology? I'd be happy to show you around the old monastery.' His husky voice was attractive, like the rest of him, and his smile was so engaging. 'Until I saw you on the boat, I imagined life would be frustrating this summer, because around here it seems that archaeologists are not a popular flavour.' There was banter in his tone, and although Melissa laughed, Andrea did not change her harsh expression.

'I'm sure you'll excuse me,' Andrea said firmly, 'but I have to get back to town. If you're not going up to the monastery just yet, Russell, perhaps you would give Nurse Harley the pleasure of your company until Gina arrives.'

'I will indeed!' His dark eyes were animated, and Melissa noted how the corners of his mouth turned up slightly when he smiled.

She found his voice attractive, low-pitched and mellow, the sound of it striking a chord in her breast. She was surprised by her reaction to him, for she was currently wary of men; but he seemed so friendly that she realised that she liked him instinctively.

'I can see I'll be able to leave you two safely together.' Andrea turned away. 'But watch out for him, Nurse, he's a real charmer.' She hurried away across the terrace to the side of the house, paused at the corner, and turned momentarily. 'When you see Gina, tell her to remain close to the house until you've had your first meeting with my mother.'

'I'll tell her,' replied Melissa, and a frown showed on her face as Andrea departed. She glanced at Russell, feeling slightly embarrassed by Andrea's treatment of him; but he was smiling, apparently unaffected by the woman's manner. He had changed out of the lightweight suit he had been wearing on the boat and had donned a black sweatshirt that clung to his upper body, revealing broad shoulders and well-formed muscles. His long legs were encased in jeans and he wore open-toed sandals.

'Andrea is a strange woman,' he mused. 'I can usually charm the birds out of the trees, but she seems to be impervious to me. She doesn't have a boyfriend that I know of, and yet there's a barrier between us — although I take comfort from the fact that she treats all men alike. Anyway, come and sit down in the shade and tell me about yourself, Melissa. I'm sure you've led a very interesting life.'

'Interesting? Yes, very interesting, but you have to be dedicated to nursing in order to survive.'

He took her elbow companionably and led her to a small iron table in a corner of the terrace. Melissa discovered that her body reacted to him as if it had a will beyond her control and seemed intent on rebelling against her attempts to quell it. She restrained her breathing before exhaling deeply, but she was slightly breathless as they sat down.

His fingers on her elbow had been gentle, and she was keenly aware that his gaze was intent on her face, as if checking her reaction to him. He was smiling, and casual friendliness exuded from him. But a wave of nervous tension surged through Melissa and she interlaced her fingers in her lap and squeezed them hard, for she was finding it difficult to resist the pull of his personality. She had to remind herself that she was an adult woman and he was not the first attractive man she had met. She forced herself to meet his gaze squarely, her expression neutral, and for a moment she seemed to succeed in controlling her rebellious senses, although the effort needed for success had been overwhelming.

He leaned his bare elbows on the table between them and lowered his chin into his cupped hands, his eyes glinting with interest. 'I expect you're finding this place like something out of a dream,' he observed. 'I know I did when I arrived. It took me a week just to get used to the surroundings. You'll get used to it all, too, before long.'

'It certainly will take a lot of getting used to,' Melissa observed.

Russell's smile faded as he spoke. 'I don't envy you in your job. I've seen Mrs Kemp, and I think she's incurable. She suffered a tremendous shock when her eldest son went missing, and I'll be surprised if she recovers from that.' He shook his head. 'It was a terrible tragedy.'

Melissa met his gaze and he held it; she could not look away. 'I don't know the facts of the case yet,' she ventured, 'but I'm always optimistic.'

She noticed how his chest and arm muscles contracted and expanded as he shifted position, and stifled a shiver. What was happening to her natural defences? He was making no effort to exert influence over her, and yet she had an uncanny feeling that he did not have to even try. He was naturally dominant, and was probably well aware of the fact. She could imagine he was watching her intently to gauge what effect he was having upon her, and she forced a smile, trying to fake a casualness she was far from feeling.

But he was completely at ease, with a naturally friendly manner. He was handsome beyond belief, and personable, but beneath the surface she noted there was a much harder quality, like polished steel, that was trying to escape from where it was imprisoned by an inflexible control.

But these were first impressions, and Melissa's mind had been inundated by many new impressions — scenery, weather, her new position, and the anticipation she was feeling about meeting her patient for the first time. She was finding it difficult to keep pace with the developments coming along thick and fast, and realised that in the back of her mind she was beginning to really worry about that first meeting with Mrs Kemp, who was the most important person in this situation. She sensed that the meeting could prove to be something of an ordeal.

'Tell about what you're doing up at the ruined monastery,' she invited Russell. 'I did some work on various digs while I was at university, and I've always been fascinated by history. If I hadn't been so enamoured with nursing at the time, I might have settled for archaeology.'

'I'll do better than tell you about it,' he responded. 'I'll take you up to the site and show you around. I'm on my way up there now, but decided to stop off here to see if you were settling in.'

'That was kind of you. But I can't leave now. Mrs Kemp is due to awaken shortly and I have to be here to start my duty. Can we make it some other time?'

'I shall look forward to it.' He nodded. 'Let me know when you can make it.'

Melissa heard footsteps along the terrace, looked round to see Gina approaching, and suffered a pang of disappointment. Russell got to his feet, smiling in a way that started flutters of uncertainty inside Melissa as he moved away.

'I hope you'll find your job straight-forward,' he remarked as he walked to the end of the terrace. 'I'll drop by later and resume our little chat, if you don't mind.'

'I don't mind,' she replied quietly, and wondered if she was tempting fate by agreeing, for he seemed to be a formidable man, and she was currently at her most vulnerable.

He waved a casual hand and leapt off the terrace onto the path below. She heard him whistling in a carefree manner as he went swinging up the path and around the villa. A sigh escaped her when the corner cut him off to her sight, because she was keenly aware that she would have liked nothing better than to have accompanied him and enjoyed much more of his company.

3

Melissa fanned her face with a hand as she considered the impression Russell had made on her in the short time they had spent together, and she was filled with wonder as she tried to analyse her feelings. No man had ever affected her so deeply, and as she turned her attention to the approaching Gina, she tried to calculate how he had managed to get through her natural defences.

'Is something wrong?' Gina's teeth glinted in a wide smile. She peered in the direction Russell had taken and nodded. 'Ah, you don't have to tell me. You've been in Russell's company. That explains everything. He has that effect on women, even me. I always feel some intangible pressure — his charisma, I should think — whenever I'm near him. Yet he never says or does anything to produce that feeling. In fact, the only woman who doesn't seem attracted to him is Andrea.'

'He's a very attractive man,' Melissa said cautiously, 'and he seems so very understanding.'

'All he talks about is the past, which is as dry as the dust he digs in up at the monastery.' Gina laughed. 'He doesn't even take any interest in the three female students who are working up there this summer.' She paused. 'I saw Gregory Lombard going along the ridge to his villa. Was he here earlier? Did you meet him?'

'Yes, I did. He's another charming man.'

'Don't be taken in by his manner.' Gina's tone was suddenly serious. 'If you want to stay happy on this island, you'll have nothing to do with Mr Lombard.'

'What makes you say that? Does he have a reputation?'

'It's not a matter of reputation.' Gina's voice took on an edge.

'What do you know about him?' Melissa asked.

Gina shook her head and turned to the villa. 'Just remember that where there's sunshine, there are also shadows. Now, it's time Mrs Kemp was awake.'

Melissa accompanied Gina into the villa and they went up to Mrs Kemp's room. Gina took a key from her pocket and unlocked the door, and Melissa followed her into the room, not quite knowing what to expect. She paused on the threshold while Gina went to the window and opened the heavy curtains. Sunlight flooded into the room, and Melissa looked around quickly, her gaze going immediately to the low bed; but all she could see was a woman's face showing above a blue silk cover.

The big window had iron bars across it, and the sight of them jarred considerably in such pleasant surroundings. Melissa noticed that there was nothing in the room that might be used to cause self-injury. She moved to the foot of the bed as Gina went to one side and reached out a gentle hand to touch the sleeping woman.

Mrs Kemp started and moaned, then opened her eyes and gazed up vacantly at the ceiling. Melissa studied the wrinkled face. Lucinda Kemp was in her late fifties. Her hair was white, and her face carried an expression of incredible sadness. But it was her eyes that arrested Melissa's attention. They were large and unblinking, practically unfocused as the woman sat up.

'Who are you?' she queried, looking at Melissa. 'What are you doing in my room?'

'This is Melissa, Mrs Kemp,' Gina said soothingly. 'She is staying at the villa for a time, and will help me take care of you.'

'I don't need anyone to look after me, thank you.' Mrs Kemp's eyes became animated and showed wariness.

'Melissa is very nice, and I like her,' Gina said cheerfully. 'I think you will too.'

'I don't like her. Tell her to go.' Mrs Kemp stared at Melissa with what seemed to be hypnotic power in her gaze.

'It's all right, Mrs Kemp, I shan't interfere,' Melissa said, and at the sound of her voice the woman shook her head. She blinked rapidly, threw back the silk cover, and attempted to rise. Gina helped her into a dressing gown, and Mrs Kemp came to confront Melissa and gazed fixedly into her face.

'Didn't I tell you she was nice?' said Gina. 'When you get to know her, she'll come and read to you. Think of the long hours you spend in this room. If Melissa is here to take care of you, then you won't be locked up for such long periods.'

'Is she locked up for long at any time?' Melissa asked.

'She is when I'm off duty.' Gina spoke over Mrs Kemp's head. 'There's been no one else to care for her.'

Melissa said nothing for a few moments, content to study Mrs Kemp, aware that she in turn was under close scrutiny by the woman. An uncanny feeling enveloped her as she probed the almost blank gaze turned toward her.

'Don't you like to leave this room, Mrs Kemp?' Melissa asked at length, and heard the hiss of Gina's sharp intake of breath.

'Please don't say such things to her, Melissa,' Gina cut in. 'She isn't allowed outside the villa.'

'She looks as if she could do with some fresh air. Why shouldn't we take her down to the beach? I'm sure she would enjoy that.'

'Mr Kemp would not permit it.' Gina led Mrs Kemp to a seat in front of the window and settled her into it, her back to the window. 'We'll get your tea now, shall we?'

'I don't want tea. I want to go to the beach.' Mrs Kemp looked at Melissa, rose from the chair and came forward to clutch at Melissa's shoulders with strong, claw-like fingers. 'They killed my son!' she screeched. 'I keep telling them he's dead, but they won't believe me. Help me get away from here. I must try to find my son.'

Gina took hold of Mrs Kemp with strong hands, overpowered her resistance, and led her back to the chair. She sat her down firmly and then came quickly toward the door, taking Melissa's arm and propelling her out of the room. Melissa went with a protest rising in her throat. She glanced back over her shoulder and saw Mrs Kemp sitting impassively, her emotional outburst apparently forgotten. Gina closed the door and locked it. Melissa looked into her worried eyes.

'What was that all about? Melissa asked. 'I fear I've not been given enough details to the background of this case. Doesn't Mrs Kemp recognise her son, or does he deliberately keep away from her?'

'It isn't Christopher she's talking about, but her eldest son Kenneth. He disappeared in the strait seven years ago. His yacht was found drifting with no sign of him aboard. The verdict was that he'd fallen overboard in a squall and was drowned. His body has never been found.'

'I see!' Melissa's brows drew together as she stifled a sigh. 'That would account for Mrs Kemp's mental condition. Poor woman! But why does she have a fixation about her son being killed? She said *they* killed him! Who did she mean?'

'According to the doctor, it's the form her insanity takes.' Gina shook her head.

'Has she had specialist treatment?'

'Yes. She was in hospital, and then spent a year in a clinic. The doctors seemed to think it was hopeless to try and restore her mental balance. They think the uncertainties of Kenneth's disappearance would have to clear before she could show any improvement. The local police were looking around for weeks afterward, but nothing ever came to light. It had to be an accidental death. What else could it be?

Kenneth had no enemies, so there was no apparent motive for murder. And who would want to kill him?'

'You've had a very difficult job here, Gina,' Melissa observed.

'I love Mrs Kemp,' Gina replied, 'and I'll do anything I can to help her, although it seems that she's never going to be well again.'

'Before I arrived I was under the impression that this would be a straightforward nursing case,' Melissa mused. 'I hadn't given any thought to the time I might have to spend here. I assumed that I'd leave as soon as Mrs Kemp's health improved, but it seems as if this could go on indefinitely.'

'Are you prepared to stay for as long as you're needed?' Gina sounded worried. 'I feel that you're the right person for Mrs Kemp. I think she'll make progress with you taking care of her.'

'We must see what the future brings,' Melissa answered. 'Obviously I'll stay as long as I'm needed, but if there's no hope for her recovery, then she should be in a nursing home where she can be cared for with all the latest nursing methods. It isn't fair to her being held here in a place that has so many bad memories.'

'I've tried to tell Mr Kemp that.' Gina shrugged. 'He doesn't listen.'

'Was there a storm the night Kenneth Kemp disappeared? He must surely have been able to swim.'

'That's why such a fuss was made when he went missing. He could swim like a fish. If he'd fallen overboard, he could easily have swum ashore, even in a storm.'

'Unless he struck his head in falling,' Melissa suggested.

'It was a calm night and he was an accomplished yachtsman. But there were reports of squalls out in the strait.'

'I get the impression that you think there was more to his disappearance than has been revealed, Gina. Was foul play suspected?'

'I don't know.' Gina's voice trembled

and her eyes narrowed, becoming shadowed with emotion. 'Nothing could be proved one way or another, but there were some peculiar things happening on the island around that time. Albania lies across the strait, and there's always been smuggling between the islanders and the Albanians.'

'And do you suspect that Kenneth Kemp was involved in such an activity?'

'No! It's more likely that he came innocently upon something that he shouldn't have seen.'

'So you think he was murdered to keep him silent? This is terrible, Gina. Poor Mrs Kemp! I really do think she should be removed from the villa.'

'Don't try telling that to Mr Kemp, for if you do, I think you'll make an enemy of him. He doesn't show emotion, but he stays here in the hope that one day Kenneth might return.'

'Is it possible that he's still alive?' Melissa asked.

'Anything is possible in these islands,' Gina asserted.

Melissa followed her down to the spacious kitchen to meet Mrs Kanera, the housekeeper, who was short and stout, with a round, olive-skinned face and piercing brown eyes. She was in her fifties, and her teeth glinted when she smiled a welcome. But she knew no English, and merely muttered something that to Melissa was unintelligible.

'She says she's pleased to meet you and hopes you'll be able to help Mrs Kemp,' Gina translated.

'I hope so too!' Melissa replied fervently.

They took Mrs Kemp's tea up to her room, and this time Melissa found herself ignored by the patient. Mrs Kemp acted as if she and Gina were alone in the room, and Melissa remained in the background, silent but observant. When the meal was finished, Gina took the tray and prepared to depart, but Mrs Kemp got up surprisingly swiftly and clutched at her.

'I want to go out!' she exclaimed. 'Take me for a walk, Gina.'

'It is forbidden.' Gina glanced at Melissa with appeal in her dark eyes.

'She'd come to no harm with the two of us accompanying her,' Melissa mused.

'I've taken her into the garden several times,' Gina said, 'but Mr Kemp says Nick has to be standing by, just in case. There's been trouble in the past. Once she broke away from us and ran down to the beach. We had to drag her out of the water. I do believe she tried to drown herself.'

'See if Nick is available now, and if he is then we'll take her out,' Melissa decided. 'She must have plenty of exercise and fresh air. It's stifling in this room, and if we're to make progress then we must ensure she's physically fit before we concern ourselves with her mental state.'

'Mr Kemp will have to be consulted first.'

'All right, I'll talk to him.'

They left the room and Gina locked the door. Melissa went in search of

Louis Kemp and located him on the terrace. He was conversing with Gregory Lombard, who seemed to be remonstrating with him about something. They both swung round at the sound of Melissa's footsteps, and Gregory smiled instantly. But Louis Kemp shook his head impatiently as if annoyed by her interruption. 'Yes, what is it, Nurse?' he demanded.

Melissa explained, and Kemp nodded without hesitation. 'Yes, yes,' he replied. 'You have full charge of my wife, so you can make any decision you feel would be in her best interests. But I would prefer you to wait until tomorrow before taking up your duties officially. I think we need to have a talk about what can and can't be done, but not right now; I'm rather busy. But you may take Mrs Kemp for a walk if Gina and Nick are able to accompany you.'

'Thank you.' Melissa turned to leave. 'I'll talk to you in the morning.'

'That will be more convenient.' Louis Kemp waved a dismissive hand. 'I'm sorry to have to put you off like this, but the pressure of work . . . ' He shrugged, leaving the sentence hanging in the air.

Melissa went back into the house and found Gina waiting. Nick was with her, and he smiled as he met Melissa's gaze and held out a hand, the dark tan of his face making his teeth seem unnaturally white. 'I'm sorry I didn't get the chance to speak to you this afternoon,' he said in English.

'He was too busy trying to catch me for throwing water on him,' Gina cut in. 'Did you speak to Mr Kemp?'

Melissa nodded. 'I'm to make all decisions concerning the care of Mrs Kemp. We'll take her for a walk now if Nick can accompany us. But I'm not to commence my duties until after we've discussed the case, which won't be until tomorrow morning. So you'll have to manage alone until then, Gina.'

'That's not a problem,' Gina said.

They went up to Mrs Kemp's room and found her standing at the barred window, peering out across the tops of the trees at the distant sea, a brooding expression on her face. She did not move when they entered the room, and it was not until Gina spoke that she roused from her reverie.

'We're going for a walk, Mrs Kemp,' Gina said. 'Let's make you look presentable.'

Mrs Kemp's dark gaze lifted to Melissa's face, but she said nothing, and Melissa remained in the background until Gina had prepared the woman for her outing. When they left the room, Gina linked her arm through Mrs Kemp's, and they left the villa to descend the steps and head onto the path through the trees. Melissa noted that Gregory Lombard and Louis Kemp were no longer on the terrace, and although she looked around cautiously she saw no sign of them.

Mrs Kemp was docile as they walked slowly along the path. Melissa walked behind the woman and Gina, and for a time she was tense and alert, but Mrs

Kemp betrayed no sign of uneasiness, apparently listening to Gina's incessant chatter. Melissa glanced over her shoulder several times but did not spot Nick, assuming that he was watching their progress while remaining unseen. They reached the beach, and when Gina suggested that they go no further, Mrs Kemp became irritable and uneasy.

'I want to walk along the beach,' she protested, pulling away from Gina.

'I think we should,' Melissa said. 'It's such a beautiful evening. It'll be quite pleasant by the water's edge.'

Gina threw her a quick glance, but nodded, and they stepped out onto the firm sand and walked down to the sea. Melissa took hold of Mrs Kemp's arm and was rewarded with a grateful glance. She clung to Melissa and began to hurry, almost dragging them along despite Melissa's attempts to curb her.

'Look at the yacht out there,' Gina commented. 'Isn't it beautiful in the sunlight?'

'Where is my son's boat?' Mrs Kemp halted suddenly and clutched at them. 'Did they find Kenneth's boat out there?'

'It was found.' Gina's face expressed concern. She glanced at Melissa. 'I think we should start back to the villa now.'

'Come along, Mrs Kemp,' Melissa urged. 'If we go back now, we can come out again tomorrow. You like coming out, don't you? It's better than being confined in your room.'

'Will you help me find my son?' Mrs Kemp clutched at Melissa's arm.

Melissa winced as Mrs Kemp's fingernails dug into the soft flesh above her elbow. She slid an arm around the woman's waist.

'No one is concerned about Kenneth,' Mrs Kemp gasped. 'He's been gone such a long time. I'm sure he's dead. I've asked, but no one will tell me anything.'

'We'll go back to the villa now.' Melissa's tone was sharp and clear. She knew she had to gain Mrs Kemp's confidence before she could begin to help her. 'If you tell me about your son, then perhaps I can help you get some answers. I know nothing at the moment, so let's go back to the villa and you can explain everything to me.'

Gina smiled and nodded her approval. 'That's right,' she said. 'Tell us about Kenneth, Mrs Kemp. You know I always try to help you.'

Mrs Kemp was silent for some moments. She gazed at the yacht, which was gleaming in the slanting rays of the setting sun. A small rowing boat was coming toward the shore from the side of yacht, and the splash of oars sounded clearly in the surrounding silence.

'There's Kenneth coming now!' Mrs Kemp spoke wildly, and pulled forward to the water's edge, her arms out-stretched, her voice echoing vibrantly as she called for her missing son.

Melissa grasped Mrs Kemp around the waist, for they were up to their knees in the sea. The woman's tense face turned toward her, dark eyes blazing with fury.

'Don't try to stop me!' she warned sibilantly. 'I won't let you stop me.'

'I don't want to stop you,' Melissa said quickly. 'Come along and we'll see who's in the boat. It's coming this way.'

Gina joined Melissa, her face taut. They managed to get Mrs Kemp back out of the water, but she struggled with prodigious strength, and they were hard put to restrain her.

'Let me go!' Mrs Kemp screamed repeatedly.

'It's all right, Mrs Kemp,' Melissa soothed. 'Just stay calm.'

'I don't want you with me anymore, Gina,' Mrs Kemp screeched. 'You're like all of them. You're keeping me from my son.' She looked at Melissa, her tone changing abruptly. 'You're new here and I trust you. Help me find my Kenneth.'

'We'll look in that boat coming ashore,' Melissa said. 'But let's walk, not run, and there's no need to get excited.'

Her calm voice seemed to be effective, because Mrs Kemp ceased struggling, and they walked to the spot where the dinghy would come ashore. Gina dropped behind and Nick came forward to join them.

Melissa could feel Mrs Kemp trembling, and looked at the figure rowing the boat. The man's back was to them, and she fancied that it was Russell Vinson. She kept a firm hold on Mrs Kemp as they paused to await the arrival of the dinghy, and as the craft drew nearer, Mrs Kemp began to cry out.

'It is Kenneth!' she exclaimed. 'It's my son coming back.' She started forward, trying to pull away from Melissa; but before reaching the water's edge, she fell and lay sprawled face down on the sand. Melissa bent hastily over her, and was dismayed to discover that she had lapsed into unconsciousness.

4

Russell sprang out of the dinghy and hurried to where Melissa was bending over Mrs Kemp. Melissa was chafing the woman's hands. Gina stood at her shoulder, blaming herself for what had happened. 'We shouldn't have brought her down here,' she kept repeating.

'She has to be made to face up to reality,' Melissa said. 'She'll never make progress while she has her present mental attitude.'

'Can I do anything?' Russell dropped to one knee beside Melissa. His shoulder touched hers, and she felt a tingle at their contact.

'I think she'll be all right in a few moments.' Melissa spoke with a tremor in her voice. 'I believe she was simply overwhelmed; she hasn't been out of her room often enough to be able to accept all the new impressions she's getting.'

'She was calling out for her son,' Russell said grimly.

'So you know about Kenneth Kemp's disappearance.' Melissa was watching Mrs Kemp's face intently, and saw her eyelids flicker.

'Andrea told me.' Russell nodded. 'No wonder Mrs Kemp is out of her mind.'

The woman moaned and stirred, then opened her eyes. She showed no sign of comprehension for a few moments. Melissa did not speak, and they waited in silence. Gina and Nick stood in the background, watching intently. Mrs Kemp finally looked at Russell, disappointment showing in her face.

'I thought you were my Kenneth,' she said tonelessly.

'I'm sorry you were disappointed,' Russell replied. 'Can I escort you back to the villa, Mrs Kemp?'

He helped her to her feet. Melissa

took hold of one of her arms and Russell supported her on the other side. The sun was going down, and shadows were closing in along the shore. It was gloomy under the trees. Melissa felt uneasy, but she had a hope of bringing about some improvement in Mrs Kemp's condition. They were silent until they reached the steps leading up to the villa.

'I'd better not come in,' Russell said. 'I have to check out the site at the monastery.'

'Do come into the villa,' Mrs Kemp said in a tone which brooked no refusal. 'My new nurse has arrived, and she'll be lonely until she settles in. She's from London, like you, Mr Vinson, and she may need some company. My own family will have no time for her, judging by the way they treated her predecessor — they drove that poor woman away!'

'Thank you,' Russell said quickly.

They ascended the steps, crossed the terrace, and entered the villa. Mrs

Kemp paused at the bottom of the stairs.

'Gina will take care of me now,' she said. 'I want to go to bed. My head aches and I need to sleep.'

'I'll give you an aspirin,' Melissa said quietly, 'and see you settled down, Mrs Kemp.'

'Gina will do that,' Mrs Kemp said obstinately. 'You can start taking care of me tomorrow, because I shall want to go out again to look for Kenneth, and one day I'll find him. I believe they're holding him somewhere against his will. But we shall find him.'

She ascended the stairs swiftly, with Gina hurrying after her. Melissa remained on the bottom stair, looking upward, until Gina had disappeared behind her mistress. Then she looked into Russell's eyes and discovered that he was watching her intently.

'This is a dreadful business,' he observed. 'I feel so sorry for her, and I doubt anything can be done for her, unless you can work a miracle.'

'I'll do what I can, but I haven't made a very good start. I fear it'll be a long business. She's been like this for years now, and that's not good.'

'If there's nothing for you to do here this evening, then why not come for a walk with me?' he suggested. 'It'll do you good to have something to occupy your mind for a spell. I have to check out the monastery; the ladies up there are complaining that someone is prowling around after dark, and it's my job to stop that sort of thing — I'm in charge of security. The moon will rise shortly and the night will be as bright as day. We could chat about the situation here, and I might be able to fill you in on some of the background.'

'I'm ready to listen to anyone who can make my job easier, but I really think I should remain here in case I'm needed.'

'Let's wait until Gina comes down,' Russell suggested.

They went out to the terrace and

watched the sun disappear behind the horizon in a spectacular display of heavenly fire. Darkness swooped in like a cloak, and the heat of the day lessened by degrees. When Gina appeared in the doorway of the villa, Melissa hurried to her side.

'I think you've made a good start, despite what happened,' Gina said. 'Mrs Kemp likes you, Melissa. But perhaps you're pushing her too hard to start with.'

'We'll see what can be done,' Melissa replied. 'But we have to be firm with her. It's the only way she'll understand.'

'I've given her two tablets and she'll sleep through the night.' Gina smiled briefly. 'You can go off now, if you want. I'll be here until you get back.'

'I need to learn as much as I can about what's been happening here,' Melissa mused. 'I'll just go up to my room and change.'

'Take all the time you need,' Russell replied with a smile.

Melissa went to put on a new dress

and shoes. She felt nervous, and when she looked at her reflection in a mirror she noted unusual glints in her blue eyes. For a moment she considered her image and wondered what it was about Russell that seemed to set up such a vibrant reaction inside her. He had strolled through her defences with no effort at all, and she trembled at the prospect of walking out with him, fearing the onset of another romantic entanglement that would have no future.

On her way out, she paused at the door of Mrs Kemp's room and listened intently, but heard no sound from within. Her thoughts were serious as she went down the stairs. She would have her work cut out for her, she knew, but she would spare no effort to succeed.

Russell smiled when she returned, and admiration gleamed in his dark eyes as he observed her appearance. They left the villa and walked through the soft, velvet-like darkness under a rising moon that created deeper shadows under the surrounding trees. A myriad of scintillating stars crowded the heavens. The perfume from the gardens thickened, and Melissa felt her senses whirl as she breathed deeply of the scented air.

'I'm not an archaeologist in the true sense of the word,' Russell said as they followed an upward path meandering to the monastery that had been well worn over the centuries. Melissa could imagine the ghosts of time prowling these lonely ways.

'I'm more the odd-job man around here,' Russell said, 'mainly in charge of security, and I have to see to the administration as well. It was a cheap way of getting here for a holiday, albeit a working one. I teach English at a sixth-form college, and I get a lot of free time at this time of year.'

'You said you might be able to tell me things that could help me handle Mrs Kemp.' Melissa's mind was on her duty. 'I assume that you know about

Kenneth, her missing son. It seems to be common knowledge.'

'I can only tell you what I've heard from Christopher Kemp, although he's never been very friendly toward me.' He laughed cynically as he added, 'Not that Andrea is any better.'

'So I can take it that Christopher's manner to me on my arrival wasn't personal! From what Mrs Kemp said, it seems they chased away the previous nurse, and Christopher was merely continuing with the treatment when I turned up. I wonder why they're against anyone helping their mother.'

'I think they act unfriendly because of what happened to their brother. There's quite a mystery surrounding his disappearance, and I haven't been able to get to the bottom of it.' He paused, and then smiled ruefully. 'Not that it's any of my business, but I have the kind of mind that loves to unravel mysteries, and when I heard the circumstances surrounding Kenneth Kemp's disappearance I just couldn't help myself — I had to delve into it.'

'And have you discovered anything?' Melissa looked round as she spoke but was unable to see much under the trees. Shadows swarmed about them as they ascended the path.

'Not much, I'm afraid, but enough to make me think that there's more to it than meets the eye. Here, let me take your arm!' He reached out swiftly as Melissa tripped and almost fell, preventing her from toppling backward down the path. 'I ought to have my brains tested, bringing you up here in the dark,' he commented.

He continued to hold her arm. Melissa shivered involuntarily at their contact, and for a moment she was drawn towards him; their faces came very close together. His features were just a pale blur in the soft moonlight. Then she reminded herself sharply that they were practically strangers and pulled away from him, although he retained his grasp on her arm.

'Are you all right?' he asked with

concern. 'We're almost there. I just want to look in on the ladies, then check around to see that nothing has been disturbed. Sometimes youths from the town, knowing there are women up here, come up with the intention of being a nuisance. If we get more trouble, I'll have to stay up here at night.'

'I'd like to come up in daylight and have a look round.'

'You said you're interested in this kind of thing.'

'Yes, I am; very much so. I like nothing better than to dig into the past.'

'So you're a kindred spirit! Although I can't imagine you in jeans and a big floppy sun hat, digging for hours under a hot sun.'

'I've found that no one ever quite fits the impressions others have of them,' Melissa observed slowly. 'Looking at you, for instance. I wouldn't take you for a teacher.'

'Really? What do I look like, then?'

'I'd say an architect, perhaps an

accountant, or something important in the City.'

Russell laughed. 'If only!'

They came eventually to the top of the hill. The ruins of the monastery were stark in the moonlight, and Melissa suppressed an involuntary shiver as the age of the place sent a ripple of emotion through her — probably a primitive fear inherited from her forebears. There was very little left except the outer walls of the ancient building, and in their centre a hut had been erected. Yellow light was shining through a square window of the temporary building, and Melissa heard the throb of a generator in the background. Off to the right were heaps of displaced soil and an area marked out with pegs and string, inside of which were traces of digging.

'I'll look in on the girls first,' Russell said. 'They might be alarmed if they hear us moving around.'

He led the way to the door of the hut and tapped loudly. It was opened by a tall, slender woman wearing jeans and a short-sleeved blouse. 'Hi, Russ,' she greeted him. 'Doing your nightly stuff?'

'Hi, Jasmine,' he replied. 'Is everything all right?'

'Nothing doing, but we live in hope.' Jasmine laughed, then saw Melissa standing behind him. 'Hullo, who have we here — another digger?'

'No, this is Melissa Harley, the new nurse for Mrs Kemp.'

'Ah, so she's arrived at last!'

'Melissa, this is Jasmine Pollard. You two should get on well together. Jasmine tells me she always wanted to be a nurse, but her father was against it.'

Jasmine held out her hand. 'I'm pleased to meet you, Melissa. I hope you'll have more luck than poor Annie Welton, the last nurse. She really needed that job, but Christopher Kemp gave her such a miserable time that she left.'

'I'm sure Melissa can stand up for herself,' Russell observed. 'You two can get together whenever you're off duty, Melissa. Jasmine will want to know the latest about what's happening in London. She's been out here two months now, and she might be able to fill you in on some of the things that have been going on around here.'

'Come and see me any time you feel like getting away from Christopher Kemp,' Jasmine invited. 'If you stand up to him and ignore the drivel he talks, then you just might survive. But he certainly makes a difficult task much harder, and his snooty sister isn't much better. No wonder Mrs Kemp is ill, having those two in the family.'

'It might be better to keep your personal thoughts to yourself,' Russell reproved her. 'I'm sure Melissa will want to make her own judgements about the people she meets around here.'

'I speak as I find,' Jasmine said forthrightly, her eyes gleaming as she gazed at Russell.

'If I do my job properly, then no one

will have cause to complain,' Melissa observed. 'The patient's interests are all that matter to me.'

'I'd like to be there if Christopher starts acting up with you,' Jasmine said.

'Come on, Melissa.' Russell laughed. 'If you hear much more of Jasmine's talk, you won't be able to sleep tonight.'

'Do come up and see us at work,' Jasmine called as they departed.

'Jasmine has a heart of gold, despite the way she runs on,' Russell said as they followed a faint path around the diggings.

There was complete silence, as if nature was brooding on the innumerable centuries it had witnessed. Melissa glanced down in the direction of the villa, saw it starkly outlined in the moonlight, and lifted her gaze across the bay far below, where Russell's yacht looked like a model set on a silver sea, its mooring lights gleaming remotely.

'It's a beautiful sight,' Russell commented, breaking into her thoughts, and she looked at him, able only to see the shadowed outline of his face. A stark question struck her — what was she doing with this handsome stranger, who had a vibrant magnetism that tugged at her awareness every single moment she was close to him? She suppressed a sigh, consoling herself with the knowledge that her work would occupy her fully when she began to nurse Mrs Kemp, and there would be no room in her mind for anything but the strictly narrow path of duty she would have to follow.

'I can see you're sensitive to these surroundings,' observed Russell softly.

Melissa realised that he was still holding her left elbow, but made no attempt to break contact. The ancient shadows around them seemed to hold many intangible ghosts of the past, and his touch was firm and reassuring.

'I hope your stay here will be a pleasant one,' he continued. 'Life is what you make it, of course, but you do have a difficult case to handle, and I wish you luck.'

'Thank you.' She was touched by his concern, and bit bottom lip as a picture of Christopher Kemp filled her mind.

'There's only one thing wrong with this paradise,' Russell said as they left the monastery and descended the path back to the villa. 'There's practically no social life on the island. A couple of night spots in town go some way to relieving boredom, but don't expect anything like what you're used to in London. After a hard day's work, it would be pleasant to be able to relax in comfortable surroundings.'

'I'm not one for gallivanting,' Melissa said. 'At the end of a day's nursing, I usually don't have much energy left.'

'You'll get at least one day off a week, surely, and I'll be around to escort you if you do feel like seeing the bright lights.' He hesitated, then continued, 'That's a genuine offer of company. I was happily married for five years, until my wife decided to have an affair. We divorced, and since then I've had no interest in women, so I wouldn't give you any trouble.'

'I feel the same,' Melissa replied hesitantly. 'I came here to forget a relationship that turned sour. I'm hoping that by taking on Mrs Kemp's problems, I'll find a cure for my own. I have no one back in England. My parents are dead, and I have no brothers or sisters.'

'So this job is a whole new start for you.' Russell tightened his grasp on her arm and she looked quickly at him to see he was gazing ahead into the shadows. 'Just a moment,' he said softly. 'I spotted a movement down the path where it forks to give access to Gregory Lombard's villa. It could be Lombard himself, or more likely Christopher; he's always running to Lombard for something or other. I'll have to check it out, but I won't stray from your side, so if you drop behind me and follow silently we can stay together and I'll see what's going on. I found this job of watching for trouble irksome at first, but now it's become second nature.'

Melissa dropped back and followed him closely as he went swiftly down the path in the direction of the villa. She glanced around somewhat nervously into the shadows, and looked along the skyline behind them in the direction of the monastery, which reared up against the silvered heavens, silently majestic and awe-inspiring in its remoteness. She inhaled deeply, savouring the scene and committing it to memory. Their feet made no sound on the leaf-strewn ground, and they soon reached the path where it forked to the left.

A man's figure was moving steadily away from them along the path. Russell stopped so suddenly that Melissa ran into him, and he turned swiftly and grasped her as she staggered. She would have fallen but for his arms around her, and her right cheek pressed momentarily against his chin as he supported her.

'Are you all right?' he whispered in her ear.

'Are you expecting trouble?' she countered.

'I'm being careful, that's all. The three women up at the site rely on me to keep them safe. I'll make another routine trip just after midnight, and again when the sun comes up. It's all part of the job, although it is inconvenient at times.'

'Is there much criminal activity on the island?'

'Enough to keep the local police busy, but there's nothing for you to worry about. I like to do my job thoroughly, and I don't really mind the inconvenience. That figure looks like Christopher Kemp going to Lombard's chalet. Those two play chess a lot, I believe.'

He held her arm as they continued down the path to the villa. Their shadows were black on the grass in front of them as they crossed a clearing in the trees, and Melissa felt herself growing taut with nervous anticipation. When they reached the front terrace of the villa, Russell stopped in the shadow of the building, and Melissa, looking up at him, could not see his face clearly.

'I hope our walk didn't bore you too much,' he said quietly. 'As I told you, there's nothing but simple pleasures around here, and I expect you'll be lonely when you've got used to the scenery. But just bear in mind that this island paradise isn't England, and don't take anyone at face value.' He glanced at the luminous dial of his wristwatch. 'It's still rather early. If you haven't had enough of my company I'd like to take you out to show you over our yacht. Professor Allen is out there, and he expressed a wish to meet you. I'm sure you'll like him.'

'Fine!' Melissa nodded. 'There's nothing I like better than a boat trip in the moonlight.'

He laughed as they continued down the path to the bay. It was darker under the trees on the lower slope, and almost as bright as day when they emerged onto the beach into the moonlight. A dinghy was pulled up on the sand, and Russell helped Melissa into it before pushing off and jumping in over the stern. He unshipped the oars and rowed steadily toward the yacht some two hundred metres out in the bay. Melissa sat in the bows, watching elusive strips of phosphorescence glinting in the displaced water.

A voice hailed them as they reached the yacht, and a dark figure materialised in the stern as Russell helped Melissa up the ladder hanging over the side.

'Is everything all right ashore, Russell?'

'There are no problems, Professor.' Melissa followed Russell into the cockpit. 'Professor Allen, Nurse Melissa Harley.'

'Pleased to meet you, Nurse,' the professor greeted her, extending a hand. 'How are you settling in at the villa?'

'Hello, Professor. It's a pleasure to be here. I take up my nursing duties in the morning, and I'm looking forward to the challenge.'

'A most difficult case, I believe,' the professor intoned. 'Come and sit in the stern. It's rather stuffy in the forward cabin at this time of night, and far more comfortable in the open air under the stars. Russell will play host and pour drinks. What are your first impressions?'

'I'm in love with the place.' Melissa laughed easily. 'It's paradise after London, and I don't think I'll miss the bright lights.'

Professor Allen laughed. 'I agree with you.' He switched on some subdued lighting and Melissa found herself looking into sharp blue eyes that studied her keenly. The professor was tall and middle-aged, and exuded friendliness. His hair was grey, and the passing years had put lines on his angular face. They chatted about local conditions before Melissa asked about the archaeological work at the monastery. Russell appeared from below with a tray of drinks.

'You've done it now, Melissa,' Russell said with a laugh. 'Start the professor off on his work and you won't get away before midnight.'

'We don't talk shop when we've left the scene of operations for the day,' Allen said good-humouredly. 'But come up to the monastery whenever you're able, Melissa, and I'll fill you in on what we're doing there.'

'What do you know about Kenneth Kemp's disappearance, Professor?' Russell asked. 'Melissa thinks that's the key to Mrs Kemp's illness.' He went on to explain what had happened on the beach earlier when he'd rowed ashore.

'It was a bad business, whatever happened,' Allen mused. 'I've heard talk, of course, but nothing definite. The only solid fact is the disappearance itself; everything else is sheer speculation. I have heard that Kenneth was murdered for being in the wrong place at the wrong time. Another theory is that he was mixed up in local smuggling and was killed out of hand over a deal that went wrong. Then there's the one about his falling overboard in a sudden squall and being washed away. I'm afraid the truth may never come out.'

'That's how I see it.' Russell handed a drink to Melissa, his face grave in the dim artificial light. His smile was sober as she thanked him.

Their conversation drifted on to other topics, and Melissa felt comfortable in the company of these two men. Professor Allen was charming and worldly, and Russell was intriguing, his appearance enhanced by the moonlight and their exotic surroundings. When Melissa glanced out across the bay, she could see a silver path of moonlight tapering away to the horizon. Such were the thoughts filling her receptive mind, that she felt she could walk along that ethereal path upward to the stars to join the illimitable number of deities abounding in Greek mythology.

Russell's voice brought Melissa's

soaring imagination plunging back to reality. 'There's a craft to seaward, Professor, which isn't showing any lights.'

Melissa looked in the direction Russell was pointing and narrowed her eyes to pick out a deceptive black shape seaward from the yacht. The anonymous vessel was moving very slowly, and glided into a bank of mist out in the strait.

'It's probably someone up to no good,' the professor commented. 'I'll call the local police and report it.'

Melissa looked toward the shore. She could see the villa on its high cliff, and to its right a smaller chalet on a lower level. Her gaze was attracted by bright lights close to the waterline under the chalet, and then she saw a small vessel moving out fast from the cliff, heading for the strait.

'There's another boat!' she exclaimed.

'That'll be Gregory Lombard's craft,' said the professor, standing at the radio. 'I'll mention it to the police.'

Russell made no comment, but Melissa, close to him, saw that he was intent on the craft. After a few moments he picked up a pair of night glasses and surveyed the fast-moving vessel, then leaned toward Melissa and spoke in an undertone.

'The professor is public-spirited,' he said. 'There's a lot of smuggling going on around the islands, and if a boat's travelling without lights, that usually means the people inside are up to no good.'

'Gina's mentioned the smuggling hereabouts,' Melissa said.

'I think you'd better take Melissa back to the villa, Russell,' Allen suggested, 'and then make your second round of the monastery. It was a pleasure meeting you, Melissa, and I hope you'll visit us again when you're off duty.'

'I've enjoyed myself immensely,' she replied, getting to her feet, aware that she was being dismissed. 'Goodnight, Professor.'

Russell took her arm to help her over the side into the dinghy. At that moment the yacht shuddered and swung fractionally, as if struck by a large wave, although the sea was flat and calm.

'What on earth was that?' Allen exclaimed.

They stood motionless, listening, waiting for they knew not what. Russell was the first to break the intense silence. 'It felt as if something struck the keel,' he said sharply. 'Now what was it, do you suppose?'

'It could have been a dolphin.' Allen's voice was dry and matter-of-fact, but when Melissa glanced at him she could see he was tense. He smiled as he met her gaze. 'I've seen a number of dolphins playing around the bay lately, and they do run into moored craft from time to time. Hurry back, Russell. There are one or two administrative items that we should take care of before we finish for the day.'

Russell smiled. 'Come along, Melissa. I'll take you back. It's your big day tomorrow, and I wish you luck with your new patient.'

Melissa climbed into the dinghy and Russell rowed her ashore. She sat tense in the little boat, looking around at the ghostly silver sea, not knowing what to expect, and half-fearing that one of those fabulous sea monsters of mythical times would suddenly surface from the placid water and hurl their frail craft and themselves to instant destruction. The atmosphere was heavy with anticipation, and she was glad of Russell's presence.

The silence remained unbroken; nothing disturbed the peacefulness of the night. Russell beached the dinghy, helped Melissa ashore, and walked her back to the villa. He squeezed her hand, then took his leave quickly, almost before she was aware of his going, and went striding off back to the beach.

She entered the villa, then closed the door and leaned against it, strangely disturbed by her thoughts. Apart from the nocturnal activity in the bay, she was up in the clouds as far as Russell was concerned. She had enjoyed his company immensely, and an eagerness to see him again throbbed deep in her heart. She was disappointed that he had not kissed her before taking his leave, though she could understand his haste in going back to the professor.

Yet there was a tiny thread of suspicion in the back of her mind that filled her with worry. Something was going on beneath the surface of everyday life surrounding the villa, the bay, and the ruined monastery. She could only hope that it would not engulf her.

5

Melissa was tired when she finally went to bed, but she discovered that sleep was almost impossible to attain. She tried to surrender to her tiredness, but as soon as she attempted to control her wayward thoughts, they slipped from her mental grasp and stampeded through her mind like a herd of runaway horses. The undercurrents she had sensed throughout the day were intriguing. She wondered at the professor's attitude when he had almost pushed her off the boat when she left, so concerned was he to be alone, no doubt to carry out some private investigation.

But her thoughts gave more importance to Russell and her reaction to him. She could still feel the strength of his attraction when they had made contact, and her thoughts were already zeroing in on their next meeting with uncharacteristic impatience. And Russell seemed keen to see her again. She tried to delve beyond his physical appearance, to glimpse the real man, but he had said very little about himself, she realised.

She was also aware that when she had met Jasmine up at the monastery, she'd had the notion that the woman seemed to be concealing some feelings for Russell. Melissa had not been aware of watching for any signs, but evidently she must have been doing so subconsciously. Her impression had come, not from any conversation that had taken place, but from Jasmine's body language — small instinctive actions and eye movements, even voice inflections. Melissa sensed that she had an interest in Russell, although nothing had been said or even hinted at.

She slept eventually, and the sun was shining in through the window when she opened her eyes again and came back to her new world. She sprang out of bed and went to the window, her heartbeat quickening when she saw the yacht anchored in the bay. The dinghy was being rowed ashore by Russell, and she watched his progress with an unblinking gaze, trying to analyse her feelings. It seemed that he had swept her off her feet, and she definitely liked him; that was all too apparent. From the first moment of their meeting, he had not seemed like a stranger, and she hoped they would be friends. If she were honest with herself, despite her current misgivings about men in general, she was aching to spend more time in the company of this fascinating person.

She turned from the window, rebuking herself strongly, and set about preparing to meet all the problems she would likely have to overcome. She went down to breakfast and found Louis Kemp alone in the breakfast room. He greeted her with a smile.

'This is a great day for me, Nurse,' he told her. 'I'm hoping you'll be able to pull my wife through this illness, though from what I've heard about that incident on the beach last evening, I do have doubts. I hope you'll be more careful in future.'

'Mrs Kemp was never in any danger, I assure you,' Melissa responded, 'and she must be taken out regularly for the physical and mental exercise she needs. If you have any concerns about how I intend to handle my duties, then you should have a doctor on call to supervise.'

'Let's see what happens when you've worked out a routine. But I must tell you, I doubt that my wife will recover — no reflection on you, of course. All I'm certain of is that the treatment plans and routines that have been tried in the past haven't worked, so there's clearly no point in repeating them. And if your nursing isn't effective, then Lucinda will have to go into a care home.'

Melissa made no reply. She was concerned about the case, and could only work on a trial-and-error basis if a doctor was not to be in attendance. She ate a frugal breakfast and then went in search of Gina, meeting her at the front door as she came in to report for duty. Gina smiled a greeting, but Melissa was perturbed to see that she was not the happy, friendly character of yesterday, and could only wonder what had happened since they had parted the evening before — an argument with Nick, perhaps. She waited for Gina to broach the subject of her problem, but nothing was forthcoming.

'Shall we go and see what frame of mind Mrs Kemp is in this morning?' Gina suggested. Her tone was flat and low-pitched.

'What's wrong?' Melissa enquired as they ascended the stairs.

'Nick is playing up.' Gina shook her head and said no more.

They entered Mrs Kemp's room. Gina drew the curtains and sunlight flooded in. Melissa stood at the foot of the bed, remaining in the background as Gina called Mrs Kemp gently and awakened her. Recalling the woman's attitude the day before, Melissa was content to watch and wait. Mrs Kemp sat up and looked around the room, speaking to Gina only to answer general questions. She looked at Melissa and gave no sign of recognition, her gaze sweeping around the room and bypassing Melissa as if she were not there.

'Say good morning to Melissa,' Gina suggested.

'I don't want to.' Mrs Kemp turned her gaze to the window. 'She'll want to make me go out this morning and I don't feel like walking. I don't want her in my room. Tell her to go away.'

'Now, you don't mean that,' Gina soothed. 'Melissa has come all the way from England to help get you better, so we must give her a chance to show how she'll take care of you. I'm sure you want to get better, don't you?'

'She can't help me. Nobody can. She can't bring Kenneth back, so she'll be wasting her time.'

'We'll get your breakfast and then see how you feel,' Melissa said. 'But first you must shower and get dressed.'

'Gina will help me,' said Mrs Kemp obstinately. 'I'm used to her.'

Melissa turned to the door. 'I'll fetch your breakfast while Gina attends to you,' she suggested. 'Then we'll plan your day. We'll only do things you'd like to do. I'm here to help you, so just tell me what you want.'

Mrs Kemp shrugged and turned away. Melissa descended the stairs on her way to the kitchen, and was confronted by Christopher Kemp. He paused and looked her up and down.

'Not wearing your uniform?' he said with a frown.

'I was advised not to,' she replied, 'on your father's instructions.'

He grinned. 'You won't last long. I expect you'll be back in England this time next week.'

Melissa shook her head, ignored him, and continued on her way. She collected Mrs Kemp's breakfast and returned to the bedroom. Gina's voice came from the bathroom as she chatted to Mrs Kemp. It seemed that their patient was in a recalcitrant mood, for Gina remonstrated with her several times before they emerged into the bedroom. Mrs Kemp shied away from Melissa like a nervous foal.

'Gina will dress me,' she said firmly. 'You can go.'

Melissa went to the window and looked out across the bay. The sea was calm, and the beach looked appealing.

'It'll be nice to take a walk along the shore after you've had breakfast,' Melissa suggested. 'It's a lovely morning.'

'The mornings are all the same to me.' Mrs Kemp's eyes glinted as she looked steadily at Melissa. 'I'm going to tell Louis that I don't want you here. The doctor doesn't call now because I refuse to see him.'

'You were happy to go along with me yesterday,' Melissa said, 'and nothing's changed since then. You'll soon get used to me being around. Now enjoy your breakfast.'

Gina sat beside Mrs Kemp and cajoled her to eat the breakfast that had been prepared. Melissa moved around the room, keeping busy and remaining in the background. When Mrs Kemp had finished the meal, Melissa again broached the subject of taking a walk.

Mrs Kemp reacted angrily. 'I am not leaving this room today,' she snapped. 'I want to go back to bed, and I shall stay there until tomorrow.'

'Leave her to me,' Gina said in an aside to Melissa. 'I'll talk her round and bring her downstairs. By then she'll have forgotten this mood and may want to go out.'

Melissa nodded and departed, and was surprised when, minutes later, Gina and Mrs Kemp descended the stairs.

'We've decided to go for a stroll along the beach,' Gina said.

'I'm going to look for my son,' Mrs

Kemp cut in. She gazed at Melissa as if seeing her for the first time. 'Will you help me?'

'Yes,' Melissa replied.

They left the villa and followed the path through the trees down to the beach. Melissa caught herself looking around for Russell; but although the dinghy from the yacht was pulled up on the sand, there was no sign of him. She assumed he was at the monastery, and forced herself to concentrate on Mrs Kemp. Gina must have guessed what was passing through Melissa's mind, for she glanced at the dinghy and then looked searchingly at her. 'Did you have a pleasant time with Russell last evening?' she asked.

'It was quiet but nice.'

'And do you like him?' Gina persisted.

'I could find nothing to *dis*like about him.' Melissa gave an account of her evening.

'So you met the students up at the monastery.' Gina nodded. 'They're very friendly. I expect you all will have a lot to talk about.'

Melissa wanted to question Gina about the existing situation between Russell and the students, particularly Jasmine, but decided against it. She would have to discover what she could without help, and she agonised over her thoughts until she forced herself to concentrate on her duties.

They had a pleasant walk along the beach, before taking the inland path back to the villa. As they passed Gregory Lombard's chalet, Mrs Kemp gazed down at the building. 'I want to ask Gregory if he's seen Kenneth today,' she said in a harsh tone. 'They were out together in Gregory's boat the night Kenneth disappeared.'

'How do you know that?' Melissa asked.

'She's rambling again,' Gina said. 'Kenneth had his own boat, and as far as I know he never went out with anyone else. When his boat was found drifting in the strait, it was deserted.'

She took hold of Mrs Kemp's arms and shook her gently. 'Don't you remember, Mrs Kemp?'

'No.' Mrs Kemp shook her head. 'It's difficult to recall anything that went on in those days. My poor head can't cope with the past.'

'Try and forget about it now,' Melissa encouraged. 'It may all come back to you if you give your mind a rest.'

A voice called to them and Melissa's heart gave a start as she recognised it. They looked round to see Russell coming along the path toward them. He was smiling, and to Melissa he looked more handsome than ever. She gazed at him critically, searching for flaws in his appearance, but saw none. She inhaled deeply, aware that the even measure of her breathing had become irregular merely at the sight of him. She recalled that she had never been as animated during her relationship with Philip Granger, and tried to analyse her feelings while Russell talked to Mrs Kemp.

When he turned his attention to Melissa and smiled a greeting, she caught her breath, a little angry with herself for permitting such a reaction, and aware of an uncontrollable spurt of emotion bubbling in her breast. He had the ability to affect her merely by looking at her, and she felt uncertain when she thought about how the future might develop.

'You seem to be coping well, Melissa,' he said. 'Mrs Kemp is quite animated.'

'She seems elated,' Melissa said. She was aware that her voice seemed a little too high-pitched for the occasion and tried to adjust it. Her heart was thudding, and she could feel her cheeks burning. Gina was watching her intently, and Melissa hoped she was not blushing like a teenager. 'This is the first time I've seen Mrs Kemp out at this time, and she appears to be enjoying herself. Earlier this morning she was worse than I thought she would be, but we're getting along better now. I'm very pleased, but keep your fingers crossed for me.'

'I will!' He nodded. 'Are you off duty this evening?'

'I'll be doing the evenings until Mrs Kemp accepts Melissa,' Gina cut in. 'So if Melissa wants time off, then evenings will be better.'

'I'll drop by the villa about seven,' Russell decided. He paused, frowning. 'That's if you fancy another stroll up to the monastery. I shouldn't be surprised if, after last evening, you hid in a corner at the thought of roaming around in the dark with me.'

Melissa nodded casually. 'I found the moonlight and the scenery enchanting,' she said. 'I'll look forward to seeing you at seven.'

'Great!' He nodded. 'If I can borrow the professor's car, I'll take you into town for a look around. See you later. I have to push on now.' He departed quickly, and Melissa gazed after him speculatively.

'He's a very handsome man,' said

Gina as they continued along the path. 'I've heard the students at the monastery talking about him. They seem to think he had a bad experience with a woman once, because he doesn't show anything other than professional interest in them. He keeps himself to himself, and only Jasmine gets a reaction from him. He talks to her all the time. She's a very nice lady.'

'It's obvious that he takes his job very seriously,' Melissa observed. 'I met Jasmine last evening, and got the impression that she was interested in him.'

'If she is, then I'd say it was one-sided, on her side. I'm sure Russell doesn't have time for any woman.'

Melissa was thoughtful as they continued. Mrs Kemp was passive, amenable to every suggestion, and it was late morning when they returned to the villa. Mrs Kemp seemed very tired as they led her upstairs to her room. She dropped onto her bed with a sigh of relief.

'Even *I'm* tired,' said Gina, sitting on a chair by the window. She smiled, but her dark eyes were filled with sadness. 'I'd like to see Nick this afternoon,' she continued. 'If you're going out tonight, I won't be able to see him later, and I need to have a serious talk with him. Usually I can catch him in the garden, but he's taking time off this week and won't be here.'

'Whatever you say,' Melissa said with a nod. 'I hope you don't have a problem, Gina.'

'There are no problems with our personal relationship. What's worrying me is his involvement with undesirables on the island.'

Gina went off before Melissa could question her further. Melissa washed Mrs Kemp's face and hands before going down to the kitchen to collect lunch. After the meal, Mrs Kemp seemed to have forgotten her earlier dislike of Melissa and settled down to sleep, but refused to take her customary tablets before closing her eyes. Melissa stayed in the bedroom until she was satisfied that her patient was sleeping soundly, and then locked the door and went down to the kitchen for her own lunch.

She was pleased with the progress they seemed to have made during the morning, but was aware that she would have to find some mind-absorbing pastimes to keep Mrs Kemp occupied and happy. She went out to the terrace and sat in the shade to relax a little, until she realised that she was watching for a glimpse of Russell and pulled herself up mentally, upbraiding herself for acting like an impressionable teen-ager.

So Russell was more handsome than average, and she was in the unenviable position of feeling unwanted and unloved — stuck in that no-man's-land of disappointment and low self-esteem which ensued from a broken romance. But that was no reason for getting excited about the first man who came into her life, she reasoned. She needed to give herself time, and breathing space, before thinking about the future. She had her hands full with Mrs Kemp, who demanded all of her attention. There was a great challenge to be faced, and only when Mrs Kemp began to make progress would Melissa be able to think of herself.

She was distracted from her thoughts by Gregory Lombard appearing on the terrace. He came to her, smiling, his eyes unblinking. 'How's Lucinda?' He dropped casually into a seat across from Melissa. 'I saw you taking her for a walk this morning, and she seemed quite happy. Is she accepting you? I should think that gaining her confidence will be the hardest part of your duties. If you can win her over to your side, you'll be able to do anything with her.'

'Yes, I'm aware of that. I've already discovered what's causing her distress. She's unable to accept that her eldest son is dead. Until we can implant that knowledge in her mind, she won't make any progress.'

'Kenneth has been dead for some years now.' Lombard shook his head. 'It's still a mystery what happened to him. He was such a good sailor, and yet he disappeared from his boat in a calm sea. There's no accounting for that.'

'I've heard several rumours about what might have happened to him,' Melissa mused, 'but I doubt the truth will ever come out.'

'I was out in the strait myself the night it happened. I didn't know he was out there, and I didn't see any sign of his boat. It was several days after he went missing before it was found. Dreadful tragedy; Lucinda is still suffering from the effects of her shock and grief. I hope you'll be able to help her. She's obviously suffering.'

'Time can work wonders,' Melissa said with a nod. 'I think I should be able to make a difference in due course.'

'Have you worked out your daily routine yet? When will you get some time off? I'd very much like to show you around. I lead a lonely life here, and I'd welcome your company.'

'Nothing's been settled yet. But I think I should be free in the evenings this week.'

'Then you must let me take you into town one evening and show you a good time.' He sounded eager, and Melissa frowned. 'What about this evening?' he continued.

'I'm sorry, but I've promised to see Russell Vinson, and he'll be calling for me at seven.'

For a moment Lombard looked unsettled, but then he smiled. 'I should have known that a beautiful woman like you would soon be snapped up, and Russell is Adonis personified. Well, he seems to be a genuine sort. Is Andrea around, do you know? I really came to see her.'

'I haven't seen her since yesterday,' Melissa said, shaking her head. 'I think she is staying in town for a few days.'

'Ah, then she'll be with Isabella.'

Gregory got to his feet. 'I need to talk to her.'

He hurried off, and Melissa frowned as she watched his retreating figure. Then she arose and went into the villa, wondering how she would pass the time until Russell arrived at seven. Anticipation was prickling in her mind, filling her with impatience, attacking the stability of her thoughts. Although she chided herself for feeling so girlish, she was unable to contain her excitement.

The afternoon wore away, the time seeming to drag. The villa was like a mausoleum. Melissa had no idea where Louis Kemp was, but she was thankful that Christopher was not around. At five she went to awaken Mrs Kemp, and entered the bedroom to find her patient awake and lying motionless in the bed, her gaze fixed on the ceiling.

'Hello. Have you been awake long?' Melissa asked. 'Did you have a nice sleep?'

Mrs Kemp started and turned her head, her dark eyes over-bright. She looked long and hard at Melissa, who began to brace herself for another session of rejection. But Mrs Kemp stirred and threw back the covers.

'I slept well, considering I didn't take any tablets,' she remarked. 'Where's Gina?'

'She had to see Nick. I expect she'll be back shortly. Can I get you something?'

'I'm thirsty. I like orange juice.'

Melissa fetched some and waited until Mrs Kemp had quenched her thirst. Then she took the glass from the woman's hand and placed it outside the bedroom. 'Did you enjoy our walk this morning?' she enquired.

'It was pleasant — better than being cooped up in this room all the time. I don't think Gina's been looking after me very well. Perhaps you should keep her away from me now you've taken over. I feel much better with you.'

Melissa was relieved. Mrs Kemp had apparently switched her focus, but she did not want Gina's usefulness to be neutralised. 'I thought you liked Gina being with you. She's devoted to you.'

'I want *you* to be with me in future. Gina's too bossy!'

'I'm sure that everything Gina does and says is for your own good.' Melissa wondered at the mood change and tried to humour Mrs Kemp. 'What do you usually do at this time of the day? I think we should stick to your usual routine as far as possible.'

'I won't do anything I don't want to do!'

'Would you like tea now?'

'Gina will get my tea! Why isn't she here?'

At that moment the bedroom door opened and Gina entered. Melissa frowned when she saw obvious signs that she had been crying. But Gina smiled and spoke in her usual cheery voice. Mrs Kemp ignored Melissa then, and grumbled and complained about being left alone with a stranger. Back to square one, Melissa thought, wondering about the mood swings affecting her patient. She realised that she probably needed a doctor to guide her through the complexities of Mrs Kemp's behavioural problems. It could become an impossible situation without a regular qualified check of symptoms.

Melissa fetched Mrs Kemp's tea and then went in search of Louis Kemp. He was in his study, engrossed in a thick ledger, but he turned to her with a smile when she entered, and listened intently to what she had to say, twiddling with a pen and nodding slowly. 'I do believe you're right,' he said at length. 'The doctor wouldn't have to see Lucinda. The sight of him would put her back considerably. But he can judge her on your reports, and observe her without her knowledge. I'll arrange for him to call and see you, and you can take it from there. What can you tell me about my wife's condition? Have you had a chance to appraise what you've seen today?'

'It's early days yet, but I think we'll make progress, and I'll be able to tell you more in a week's time. I'll monitor Mrs Kemp carefully, and when I've spoken with the doctor we'll have a much better idea of what to do and how it will affect her.'

'I leave it in your hands. I'm sure you're moving in the right direction. Are you finding my wife easy to handle?'

'She has to be led, not driven. I'm sure she'll be more comfortable and easier in her mind when I've established a suitable routine for her.'

Melissa left it at that and went back to Mrs Kemp, finding her in bed with her clothes on and Gina pleading with her, trying to get her to undress. When Melissa entered the room, Mrs Kemp threw back the covers and put her legs out of bed.

'I want to go for a walk,' she said firmly. 'I wanted to talk to Gregory Lombard this morning about Kenneth but didn't get the chance, so I want to see him now.'

'I was talking to Mr Lombard a short

time ago,' Melissa said. 'He came to see Andrea, and when I told him she was staying in town he hurried off to see her. I'm afraid you'll have to wait until tomorrow morning, but we'll definitely call on him then. I'm sure he won't be back today.'

Mrs Kemp gazed at Melissa for some moments, her gaze unblinking, and then she nodded and got back into bed. Gina undressed her without resistance, and Melissa sighed silently in relief as they left the room.

'She'll be all right now,' Gina said, glancing at her watch. 'You'd better get moving and change for your date. Russell will be on time, and you won't want to keep him waiting.'

'Perhaps I should wait a couple of days before taking time off,' Melissa mused. 'This is my first day on duty, and I wouldn't want anyone to think I'd rather slack off than do what I'm here for.'

Gina shook her head. 'Get away now and enjoy yourself. There's another day tomorrow, and Mrs Kemp will still be here with all her problems. Apart from that, I may need some time off myself in future, and then you'll be stuck on duty for hours with no one to relieve you. It looks like being a matter of give and take, so off you go without another word. I'll look in on Mrs Kemp from time to time, but we won't hear another thing from her until the morning.'

Melissa felt some misgivings as she departed, but she had to start as she meant to go on. She went to her room, filled with a spate of conflicting emotions. She wanted to see Russell again, despite her mind warning her that she could be heading for trouble. But she seemed to have lost the edge to her customary determination, feeling as if she did not care about the future so long as she could continue to see this extraordinary man.

6

Melissa had mixed feelings as she surveyed her reflection in the long mirror in her bedroom. She tucked in a stray tendril of blonde hair that had escaped her French pleat, her thick fringe giving her blue eyes a tinge of mysterious allure. She adjusted a strap of her white cotton dress, swished her hips gently, and nodded in approval at her small waist. She had been doubtful about wearing her white strappy high heels, remembering the path through the trees to the monastery; but Russell had mentioned borrowing the professor's car and taking her into town, so she had to be prepared. She checked her make-up for flaws, nodded, and smiled at her wide-eyed image. 'You'll do, Melissa!' she commented, and hoped Russell would agree when he saw her.

She picked up her filmy shawl and clutch bag and went out to the terrace, humming softly as anticipation soared through her like a flight of swallows. It was just before seven, and she felt torn by her desire to meet Russell and the common-sense part of her that wanted to hold off and compel her to act reasonably. But she could find no excuse for not following her inclination. She did not have to do more than pass the time with him. Yet in the back of her mind was the fear of being over-whelmed by a grand passion that would sweep her along as if she were in the grip of a tsunami. She did not know if the change in her natural attitude was caused by her exotic surroundings or the pull of Russell's magnetism. All she knew for certain was that she had waited quite impatiently all day for this moment to arrive, and nothing but the sight of Russell would assuage her heightened feelings.

She stepped on to the terrace, fully expecting to have to wait for Russell's arrival, and was surprised to see him seated at the little table in a corner of the terrace, looking as if he had been there quite some time. He stood up at the sight of her, a smile of welcome on his lips. Melissa's heart warmed as she went to him, aware that the niggling impatience that had tortured her all afternoon had miraculously vanished. She heaved a sigh of relief and accepted the fact that she had developed a passion for him — a growing infatuation that held her with inflexible bonds; and all she could do was hope it would pass eventually and permit a return to normal.

'Hello,' he greeted her. His eyes were bright with admiration as he took in her appearance. 'I don't know about you, but I thought today would never end. How did you get on with Mrs Kemp? I've been wondering about you, seeing this was your first day, but you seem to be still in one piece.'

'It passed quite well.' Melissa hoped her voice was steady, but feared her feelings would show in her face. Russell was wearing a light grey suit with a matching tie, and looked refreshed and animated. She gave him a brief rundown on her day.

'I'm sure you're having a good influence on Mrs Kemp,' he observed.

'She seemed to do quite well this morning. But she's subject to mood swings. She had a period of not wanting me around, and then switched against Gina and wanted her off the premises. I know it's too soon yet to make any kind of decision about her, but I'm beginning to wonder whether I'll really be able to help her. I've asked for a doctor to be brought in to guide me, and it will be up to him to form a considered opinion.'

'And what will happen if you can't help her?'

'Mr Kemp may decide to put her in a clinic for further treatment, and I'd be out of a job.'

'I hope it won't come to that.' He frowned. 'You've only just arrived.'

Melissa's gaze lingered on his features, and she liked what she saw. He shook his head, took hold of her elbow, and walked her to the terrace steps. They descended to the path in silence. Russell's grip on her elbow was firm, filling her with excitement.

'Let's change the subject,' he said. 'I have the professor's car for the evening but I have to check the site at the monastery before we can drive into town.'

'That sounds fine to me,' Melissa told him.

She sighed with relief as they ascended the path, for her mental turmoil eased with each step she took. Just being in Russell's company relieved all the pressure that had assailed her during the day. Her left elbow was tingling where his fingers gripped her, and his nearness tugged at her awareness. She felt light-hearted, and began to hope the evening would never end.

Her sense of euphoria faded when they reached the site and she saw

Jasmine standing in front of the hut, apparently waiting for Russell's arrival. She was wearing a dark blue dress and white sandals. 'Hi, there, Russ!' she called as they approached. 'I've been waiting for you to show up. I heard you say this afternoon that you had the use of the professor's car for the evening, so you can give me a lift into town.' She smiled cheekily at Melissa. 'I can make my own way back later.'

'No trouble,' Russell said instantly. He glanced at Melissa. 'It's just as well we decided to go in that direction.'

'I'm not intruding, am I?' Jasmine asked. 'I could ask Gregory Lombard for a lift. He's always ready to be of service that way.'

'You're no trouble at all,' Russell replied. 'Why don't you two start walking down the back path while I check up here? I'll catch up you before you reach the car. You know where the professor leaves the car, Jasmine?'

'Sure.' Jasmine smiled. 'Come on, Melissa — there's a path over this way that'll take us directly to the road to town.' She set off, with Melissa following her.

As they walked, Jasmine asked, 'How did you get on with Mrs Kemp today? I wondered how you were doing. I wouldn't have your job for a thousand pounds a week. And living under the same roof with Christopher Kemp would be the pits. I've seen him prowling around the monastery at odd times — the place is on Kemp property — but I always dodge him when I can.'

They chatted casually as they followed a winding path that led off to the left of the one Melissa and Russell had used to reach the monastery. Jasmine was a cheerful woman, high-spirited, and always ready with a smile and a joke. As they reached a metalled road, where a big car was parked in a lay-by, she looked round for Russell, and pointed out his figure above them as he came plunging down the path.

'How are you getting along with

Russ?' Jasmine asked. 'He takes his job very seriously here; nose always to the grindstone. Nothing seems to distract him from his work. He doesn't seem to mind the loneliness of this place, while I sometimes feel I'm losing all sense of reality, digging into the past every day. I don't know why I ever thought it would be a good idea to spend a summer here.'

'You could leave if it gets too much,' Melissa suggested.

'I don't mind it really, so long as I can get into town now and again. Don't you think Russ is too handsome? He's so good-looking, and I think that's wasted in a man. I wouldn't mind having his nose, though. I don't know what's wrong with mine. It looks as if my mother sat on me when I was a baby.'

Melissa laughed as she inspected Jasmine's nose. 'I don't see anything wrong with it,' she remarked.

'Well, you're another who is flawless. You and Russ go well together! It must be wonderful going through life knowing you couldn't improve your appearance in any way. Have you left a boyfriend or a husband back in London?'

'Only an ex-boyfriend.' Melissa firmed her lips against further remarks.

'Ah! I know the feeling. You have my sympathy. It's like the end of the world has come, isn't it? But the misery soon passes. The secret is to keep an open mind and look forward to the future. You're in the right job to help you get by. You'll take on Mrs Kemp's health problems and lose yourself in trying to solve them.'

Melissa found herself liking Jasmine. The woman was an eternal optimist, and apparently did not have a care in the world. Russell arrived then and produced the car keys.

'You get in front with Russell,' Jasmine said to Melissa. 'You're his date. I'm just a hitchhiker.'

'Are you meeting someone in town, Jassy?' Russell asked when they were driving around the bay.

'No one in particular. I would have asked you to take me out this evening if you hadn't made a date with Melissa. You're much too popular for your own good, Russ. Being in great demand could inflate your ego, and that's not healthy for a man.'

Melissa smiled. 'I hope my arrival hasn't ruined your plans,' she said to Jasmine.

'Take no notice of the way she talks,' Russell cut in. 'She's just trying to make you feel guilty. I took her out last week and vowed I wouldn't get trapped again. She nearly got us arrested.'

Jasmine laughed merrily and winked at Melissa. 'You've got to have a good time while you're young,' she said.

'And you certainly believe in living life to the full,' Russell added.

Jasmine chattered cheerfully, and in no time at all they were entering Pargos. 'Where do you want to get out?' Russell asked Jasmine as he drove slowly along the main street that led to the quay.

'That restaurant on the corner by the church will do.' She began to open the car door. 'Have a nice time, you two,' she said as the car stopped. 'See you tomorrow, Russ.'

'Be careful,' he warned.

'You worry too much!' Jasmine alighted from the car and was gone in a flash.

Russell shook his head. 'You can see the kind of person she is,' he said. 'Now, shall we take a look around? Later I'd like to take you for a meal. How does that sound? I'm afraid there's nothing more exciting to do around here.'

'I'll look forward to it.' Melissa was aware that she had not eaten much during the seemingly long day.

Russell parked the car on the quay and they alighted. There were no ships moored to the quayside, and the town looked as if it were sleeping, lulled by the evening sunshine. The sun was low on the horizon, the bay calm, the sky cloudless, and the air was laced with the scent of the flowers and trees that abounded.

'There isn't much to do except admire the scenery,' Russell said. 'There's a larger town along the coast with more amenities, but it's too far to travel for an evening. We'd really need to spend the day there to do it justice.'

'I'm quite happy with this,' Melissa told him.

They strolled around the town, and Melissa was quite taken by the brooding atmosphere. She had to tell herself that she was really in Greece, and could still not quite believe it. Her thoughts turned to Mrs Kemp as she looked around. She hoped she would be able to improve the woman's health.

Russell was familiar with the town and explained some of its history. Melissa listened intently to what he had to say, but it was the timbre of his voice rather than his words that held her attention. She hoped he would hold her arm, but he strolled along quietly at her side.

'I'm afraid that's all,' he said at length. 'Not much for a Londoner.'

'I'm not missing London,' she told him. 'I have too much work to do to worry about my surroundings. But I love Greece. I think it's wonderful.'

'I know what you mean. I wouldn't have missed this for anything. I'm so glad I had the opportunity to come.'

Melissa was not sorry when it was time for them to visit the restaurant, which was situated on the main street overlooking a small market square. Entering, she looked around for Jasmine, expecting to find her there with a cohort of young men, but there was no sign of her. Russell led her to a corner table by a back window overlooking the bay. There were several customers at the surrounding small tables, mostly young couples out for the evening. Russell seated Melissa and then sat opposite. He leaned towards her.

'Stephanos owns this place. He's a lovable character, and his cuisine is out of this world. His mother will tell your fortune from your coffee cup.'

'Really?' Melissa was intrigued.

'It's a tradition here. The coffee doesn't dissolve. You turn your cup upside down, and Stephanos's mother reads the coffee grounds, if you're interested in that sort of thing. I've had a meal here several times. As you can see, the place is spotless. Are you hungry?'

She nodded. A tall man dressed in the black suit of a head waiter approached them, carrying menus. He bowed, smiling, and addressed Russell in good English. 'Welcome,' he greeted them. 'You are here again, so I hope it is because you found our food to your liking.'

'It was perfect,' Russell replied. He took the menus that were proffered and handed one to Melissa with a smile. 'Do you understand Greek?' he asked.

'I'm afraid it's all Greek to me,' she countered with a grimace.

'Very good. I must remember that. If you'll rely on my choice, I'll order for you. The last time I was here I had moussaka, which was delicious, and you must certainly try it if you're not vegetarian. It's the Greek national dish.' He glanced up at the attentive Stephanos. 'We'll start with Avgolemono soup. It'll be perfect for an English lady's first taste of Greek food.'

'Moussaka sounds good,' Melissa said. 'If the Greeks like it, then I'm sure I will too.'

Russell ordered their food and a bottle of red wine. Stephanos wrote down the order. 'And we'll have kataifi for dessert,' Russell said, then turned to Melissa and explained, 'It's a pastry rolled with nuts and honey and sprinkled with syrup. That should do for your first Greek meal, and we can have coffee later.'

Stephanos departed and Russell leaned his elbows on the table. He looked intently at Melissa. 'Excuse me for staring. But the sea this morning was the exact colour of your eyes — very pale blue, with depthless warmth.'

'Flattery will get you everywhere,' Melissa responded. 'No wonder Jasmine wanted your company this evening — every woman loves a flatterer.'

He glanced around as if seeking Jasmine, and a frown touched his forehead. His face sobered for a moment, and Melissa, watching him intently, wondered what was passing through his mind. Was he thinking that he would rather have been with Jasmine than with his present companion? She stifled the thought instantly, determined not to ruin the mood.

When their meal arrived, Melissa found it very much to her taste. Russell, watching her, nodded. 'You seem to like it,' he said. 'I'm so glad.' He glanced at his wristwatch. 'We have plenty of time. I don't have to check out the monastery until much later, and the way you dress to go out, I must think twice about dragging you all over the island. I think the trouble with me is that I've forgotten how to treat a lady.'

'You haven't put a foot wrong so far,'

Melissa said with a smile.

She could not remember a time when she had enjoyed better food. The moussaka was cooked to perfection, and the pastry of the dessert seemed to melt in her mouth. After she had finished, she leaned back in her chair and sighed contentedly. 'That was splendid,' she observed. 'About the best meal I've ever had.'

Their coffee arrived, and as they were finishing, a grey-haired lady, short and of ample figure, approached their table and spoke in Greek.

'Stephanos's mother,' Russell said. 'She wants to know if you'd like to have your fortune told.'

'I don't think so, not this evening,' Melissa said quietly. 'I'm just a little bit apprehensive about what I might hear. Perhaps the next time I come.'

'It's just a bit of fun,' Russell said. 'You don't have to take anything she says seriously.'

'I'll make a point of having my fortune read the next time I'm in,'

Melissa promised.

Russell relayed the message and they prepared to leave. Stephanos appeared with the bill and Melissa reached for her bag. 'It's my treat,' Russell said quickly, producing his wallet.

'Only if I'm allowed to pay the next time,' she countered.

Russell smiled and nodded. 'In the not-too-distant future,' he said with a smile, and Melissa agreed.

They returned to the lay-by where the car had been parked, and the last of the day was fading into oblivion as Russell took a torch from the car and then locked its doors. 'Have you had enough of my company for one day?' he asked.

'If you're going up to the monastery again, I'll come along,' she said, not wanting her time with him to end. 'I don't feel like calling it a day just yet.'

'You must be a glutton for punishment,' he observed. Under the trees, he took hold of her arm. She quivered and he noticed. 'Are you cold?' he asked.

'Not at all.' She longed to tell him the truth — it was her reaction to his touch.

They lurched several times on the uneven path, their shoulders making contact. Russell slid an arm around Melissa's waist and pulled her closer. She felt her pulse begin to race. She drew a quick breath and let her weight sag against him, as if she were losing her balance.

'Maybe it wasn't such a good idea to bring you up here at this time of night,' he said. 'You've had a long day.'

'But the evening certainly raced by,' she observed.

'Yes, didn't it?' He paused. 'That's a good sign — or is it?'

The next instant he was embracing her, and Melissa stifled the instinctive protest that rose in her throat. His arms were like rigid steel bands around her slender body, holding her motionless, and she had the feeling that she was teetering on the edge of a precipice. Her hands clutched at him, seemingly of their own volition. She raised her face, sensing that he was about to kiss her, and his searching lips touched her ear before moving swiftly to her mouth, evoking a riot of sensation and pleasure as they fastened onto her lips with the precision and power of a striking bird of prey.

They swayed together, and might have fallen if Russell's right elbow had not rested against the trunk of a dark pine. Melissa shuddered with intense pleasure. Their mouths melded together, his kiss surprisingly gentle, as if seeking permission to press on to complete fulfilment. She yielded to him, feeling as if she were sinking into a perfumed sea that closed around her with wavelets of sheer delight. His tongue entered the sweet, warm depths of her mouth, their lips compressed, and a slow urgency built up in her as their contact became more urgent. She could smell the intangible scent of him, and was inflamed by the urges assailing her.

Her breath was warm against his

cheek. He held her as if she were made of fragile china, his head moving slightly to stroke his lips against hers in a slow, erotic caress that set her tongue and lips afire with a fervent need for more. Melissa opened her eyes and looked up at him, but could see nothing through the shadows surrounding them. She thought of the long hours of the afternoon that had tortured her with their slow passing, and now she was in his arms — this man who had attracted her with his magical presence — and she felt at peace, at one with him.

It was Russell who eased back and drew a deep breath, his arms still holding her as she gasped, feeling the need for more. 'Hey, I'm sorry!' he said huskily, his low-pitched voice unsteady. 'It was just a natural reaction. You fell against me, and it happened before I realised what I was doing.'

'Don't make a big deal of it,' she said instantly. 'I liked it.'

'You did?' He sounded surprised, and Melissa laughed softly.

'Why not? You're a very handsome man. What's a kiss between friends?'

He looked at her for several moments, his face just a pale blur under the trees. He was still holding her arms. 'In that case,' he said slowly, 'I should like to do it again.'

'I won't stop you!' She was shocked by the abandonment sounding in her voice.

He laughed and drew her into his embrace, and this time he did not act from a natural impulse. He kissed her as she had never been kissed before. Melissa felt weak; her knees trembled, and she was thankful he was supporting her. When they broke apart for air she leaned her face against his shoulder, not wanting the moment to end, and he stroked her cheek, his chest rising and falling powerfully against her breast.

He stiffened suddenly, lifted his head, and appeared to listen intently. Melissa looked around, feeling as if she were rising from the depths of the ocean.

'Did you hear that?' he demanded. 'It

sounded like a cry.'

'I didn't hear anything.'

He stepped away from her, turning his head slightly and listening intently. 'There it is again.' His voice was suddenly sharp and commanding. 'Follow me, Melissa, and stay close.'

He turned abruptly and ran up the path toward the monastery. Melissa, gasping for breath and unsteady, was suddenly afraid of being left alone in the crowding shadows and followed him quickly. She paused to pull her sandals from her feet and carried them as she followed his dark, elusive shadow through the trees.

They reached the hut at the monastery. Yellow light was blazing through the doorway — the door stood wide — and two figures were standing just outside, peering into the shadows.

'What's happening?' Russell called as he raced forward. The two figures were feminine, and both were gazing down the slope.

'Thank heaven you're here, Russell,'

one of them said quickly. 'We heard a woman's voice shouting down that path to the road, and it sounded like Jassy.'

'Wait here, Melissa,' Russell spoke sharply as he ran headlong down the slope. His figure vanished beneath the trees, and they heard him calling Jasmine's name.

Melissa could see nothing in the shadows. She listened intently to Russell's voice becoming more distant. One of the girls turned to her. 'You're the new nurse at the villa, aren't you?' she queried.

'Yes. I'm Melissa Harley.'

'I'm Sheila Hesp, and this is Doreen Kerry. Jassy was talking about you earlier. She went with you and Russell into town this evening, didn't she?'

'We drove her in, dropped her off, and didn't see her again.'

'And she was probably picked up by someone who turned nasty,' Doreen observed.

'Here's Russell coming back — and someone's with him,' said Sheila.

'It sounds like Jassy.' Relief sounded in Doreen's voice. 'Let's hope she's all right.'

Melissa heard Jasmine laugh, and relief filled her as well. She went forward to the two figures coming up the slope. 'What was wrong?' she called.

'It's all right,' Russell said. 'Jasmine got herself into a hole she couldn't get out of.'

Melissa frowned. Jasmine laughed, but she sounded shaky.

'Someone's dug a hole down there on the path and covered it with branches,' Jasmine said breathlessly. 'I stood on the branches, went through them, and found myself in a hole over my head. It's a good job you heard me yell, Russ. I could have been trapped down there all night.'

'That hole wasn't there when we went out,' Russell said. 'We walked over that path on the way down to the car and it was all clear.'

'So someone's played a joke on us.' Jasmine's voice was suddenly serious.

'A very poor sort of a joke,' Russell observed. 'You might have broken your neck.'

'Who would have done such a thing?' Melissa mused.

'There's only one man around who isn't happy with us working up here.' Jasmine's face was just a pale blur in the shadows.

'I don't think Christopher Kemp would go as far as that to make us leave,' Russell said.

'I wouldn't trust him an inch,' asserted Jasmine.

Melissa frowned. 'That doesn't make sense. But then, he *was* deliberately rude to me when I arrived, and I've heard that he made the previous nurse's life such a misery that she left.'

'Not to worry,' said Jasmine, the usual cheery note back in her voice. 'All's well that ends well. Did you two have a nice evening in town?'

'Most enjoyable,' Russell said.

Melissa, thinking of the kiss that had been interrupted by Jasmine's mishap, felt as if she had been robbed of a great emotional experience.

'I'd better get you back to the villa, Melissa,' Russell said. 'Jasmine, you'll have to take better care of yourself after this.'

'I'm all right,' she protested. 'Hey, I didn't dig that hole on the path, and I didn't fall into it intentionally!'

Russell ushered the students into their hut and closed the door. Then he took Melissa's arm and they descended the path to the villa.

'Have there been other incidents?' Melissa asked.

'Not as bad a hole dug and covered over,' Russell replied. 'But odd things have happened. Don't pay any attention to what Jasmine said about Christopher. I would think it was more likely that some Greek man she led on a bit decided to play a trick on her. She always uses that path after dark.'

'What kind of a man would play a trick like that?' Melissa wondered aloud.

They reached the villa, and when they approached the front door a man stood up at the little table on the terrace and came forward. It was Professor Allen. 'I apologise for intruding,' he said. 'Please forgive me. I've been waiting for you to return, Russell. A problem has arisen and we must attend to it immediately. Would you come with me now?'

'Certainly, Professor.' Russell turned to Melissa. 'Thank you for such a wonderful evening. I enjoyed it tremendously. Forgive me for rushing off like this; I'll see you tomorrow. Goodnight, Melissa.'

'Goodnight,' she responded, and suppressed a sigh as a feeling of desolation infiltrated into her happiness at the thought that their evening had come to an end.

The professor was already moving off the terrace. Russell leaned forward and kissed Melissa's forehead before hurrying after him, leaving her gazing after them, shocked by the abrupt change of situation. She had been looking forward to another intimate, leisurely kiss instead of a peck on the forehead, and her heightened emotions subsided like a pricked balloon as she turned and reluctantly entered the villa.

7

Melissa slept deeply, exhausted by her long day, and awoke early the next morning to find the sun shining into the room. She arose instantly and went to the window to look at the professor's yacht. A sigh escaped her at the sight of it, riding serenely at anchor on a perfectly blue sea. She recalled Russell's description of her eyes, likening them to the sea on the previous morning.

She leaned her elbows on the windowsill and gazed dreamily into the distance, recalling the salient points of the previous evening. The memory of Russell's kiss made her squirm. Then Jasmine's experience stabbed through her mind and she straightened, frowning as she recalled the site at the monastery, the shadows and the figures in the deceptive starlight.

It was incredible that someone

should dig a hole in the path and cover it over to deliberately catch some unfortunate person. Or had it been done to catch a specific person? Melissa sighed again and looked for the dinghy that Russell used to get back and forth from yacht. It was drawn up on the beach, and she glanced eagerly along the path, checking its meandering course all the way up to the monastery but without catching sight of him.

When she went down to the dining room for breakfast, she found Christopher seated alone at the table. He looked up at her and smiled crookedly, his eyes filled with an over-bright stare. 'How is our charming nurse this morning?' he asked.

'Very well, thank you.' She wondered if he knew anything about the trap on the path. Someone might have been seriously hurt, and although Christopher seemed antisocial, she could not believe he would plan to injure someone deliberately.

'What are your plans for my mother

today?' His smile vanished and his eyes became wary as he awaited her answer.

'I shan't know until I see how she is feeling. If she doesn't want to walk today, I'll have to find some other way to occupy her. I'll work out a routine that'll be beneficial for her. We need to rekindle her interest in life and ease her out of her introspection.'

'You'll be wasting your time, whatever you do. The doctor knows my mother is a hopeless case, but my father won't accept the obvious, hence your presence here. But he'll come round to facing the truth eventually, and then you'll be out of a job.' He smiled. 'I'm not against you personally, you understand. It's just that I can see the futility of your efforts. What you are doing is a complete waste of time.' He shrugged. 'But I suppose it's all right if it gives my father some sort of hope.'

Melissa breakfasted and departed, leaving Christopher reading a newspaper. She went up to Mrs Kemp's room and found Gina dressing the patient for breakfast. Melissa frowned when she saw Gina's face. She looked as if she had not slept at all during the night, and she seemed dull and listless. Melissa was appalled, and placed a hand on Gina's shoulder.

'Can you tell me about it, Gina?' she asked.

Gina's eyes filled with tears and she shook her head. 'There's nothing to tell,' she replied. 'Nick will have to change his ways if we want to stay together, but it seems he isn't prepared to do that. So I've got no choice but to leave him, and it'll be all over between us.'

'I'm so sorry, Gina. You two were very happy just two days ago. What happened?'

'I don't want to talk about it, Melissa. You're very kind, but there's nothing to be done.'

'You said Nick was mixed up with some undesirables. Is that the trouble?'

Gina hesitated, her expression showing indecision. Then she nodded. 'Yes.

169

Nothing I can say or do will make him change his mind. It's his decision.' She dabbed at her eyes with a handkerchief and drew a deep breath. 'What shall we do with Mrs Kemp this morning?'

'We'll take her walking and use a different route from yesterday. How about going up to the monastery to watch the students digging?'

'That's a good idea! I've taken her up there before, and she likes to watch them at work; it seems to quieten her. I'll fetch her breakfast, and then we can make an early start.'

Melissa sat with Mrs Kemp, watching the woman while wondering what was going on in the shadows of this sunny island. What would she find if she could turn over the stones of everyday life and look beneath them? And who would be involved in that underworld?

Even Russell looked somewhat grim at odd moments, as if he had a lot of worry on his mind and was finding it difficult to conceal it. Jasmine, too, seemed too good to be true — acting as the life and soul of the ancient archaeological site, but apparently sharing some secret knowledge with Russell: for Melissa had noticed their occasional glances at each other, although she had tried hard not to read significance in them.

When Mrs Kemp was ready, they set out to walk up the path to the monastery. Gina linked arms with Mrs Kemp and Melissa walked behind, not wanting to crowd her patient. She listened to Gina talking animatedly and Mrs Kemp answering occasionally, giving her hope that this therapy was having a positive effect.

When they passed the tree where Russell had kissed her, Melissa caught her breath as she was overcome by a rush of emotion that bubbled up inside her. Their contact had been so powerful that it had erased the residue of grief remaining from her shattered romance. Now she felt liberated from the past — but what of the future?

When they reached the ruins, Melissa

looked around eagerly for Russell, and was disappointed when she did not see him. The three students were busy uncovering traces of the past, and Professor Allen was looking at some diagrams on a table beside the hut. He heard Gina's voice and straightened, smiling when he saw his visitors. He came forward eagerly.

'Dear Mrs Kemp,' he said cheerfully. 'I'm so pleased to see you. Melissa is certainly up to her duties. I've long thought that you should be taken out and given some interest in life. Can I show you what we've been doing here, and what we hope to find?'

'Thank you, Professor,' Mrs Kemp replied. 'You can talk to Melissa and Gina. I'll chat with Jasmine.'

Gina accompanied Mrs Kemp to the spot where Jasmine was crouching in a shallow trench, intent on carefully brushing dirt aside in her search for relics of the past.

'Did Russell tell you about the trap that had been dug on the path,

Professor?' Melissa asked. 'Jasmine fell into it, and it's a wonder she wasn't seriously hurt. Isn't Russell up here today?'

'Yes, he told me about the trap; and no, he isn't here this morning. He's gone into town to talk with the local police. What happened last night is too serious to be ignored. I'd never forgive myself if one of the girls was injured.'

'Who do you suppose would have done such a thing? Have there been other incidents of a similar nature?'

'I'm sure I don't know,' Allen answered, shaking his head. 'Russell hasn't reported anything. He's in charge of site security and takes his duties very seriously. That trap was dug while you were in town, and the path is the one we usually take to get to and from the beach. Russell often uses the path by the villa because he likes to check the whole area, and someone must have worked very hard to complete that trap before you returned from town.'

'Is someone trying to prevent your work from continuing?' Melissa asked.

'I honestly don't know. I can't think why anyone would object to what we're doing.'

'The monastery is on Kemp property, isn't it?'

'That is correct, and my society arranged for us to come here this summer. Louis Kemp was most keen to have us do the work.'

Melissa suppressed a sigh. She saw Mrs Kemp drop to her hands and knees beside Jasmine and begin to dig into the earth with her fingers. 'I'd better remove my patient before she gets too involved,' she observed.

'Before you go, I'd like to warn you about getting too friendly with Russell,' the professor said.

Melissa glanced at his face and saw that his jaw was clenched and his face set in a grimace, as if he had something unpleasant to impart. She frowned.

'I don't know how to put this,' he continued, 'but I think it should be said. I'm afraid that if certain people, who shall be nameless, see you on friendly terms with Russell, they might think you're using your job as a nurse to cover your real purpose for being here, which they will believe is to spy on them. They're ruthless men, and might take steps to remove you.'

Melissa gasped and her eyes widened. 'I'm afraid I don't understand what you're saying, Professor,' she said. 'I'm just a nurse, and I have no ulterior motive.'

Allen shrugged. 'I know that, of course, but those people don't. To them, all strangers are suspect. Why do you suppose Kenneth Kemp disappeared as he did? I think he was in the wrong place at the wrong time and was removed. He was practically a stranger here in those days. So that's why I think you should be very careful, Melissa.'

'Thank you for the warning, although I don't understand what it's about. What of Russell? Is he involved in some covert activity against those unknown men you mentioned?'

'Not to my knowledge. He came to us with impeccable references. But it's to do with smuggling, which has been going on around these islands for centuries, and it's big business in these parts. I'm afraid you've come here at a very delicate time, and you could get caught up in something serious if you're not careful. I'm warning you because you should be aware that there's danger here.'

'I'll be very careful,' Melissa said. She thought about Russell and Jasmine, and her suspicion that something was going on between them under the surface of everyday life seemed to take on another dimension. Were they involved in smuggling? She heaved a sigh. 'Thank you, Professor. I'll bear in mind what you've said. Now I'd better get Mrs Kemp out of there.'

She hurried forward and took Mrs Kemp's arm. 'It's time we were going,' she said, and Mrs Kemp made no protest as they led her away. They took the alternative path down the slope toward the villa, and stopped when they came to the spot where the trap had been dug. It lay open and exposed now, looking innocuous in the bright sunlight, but Melissa recalled the sinister shadows of the night before and felt a tremor of fear trickle through her.

They went on and, when they reached the spot where the path branched to the right to pass above Gregory Lombard's chalet, Mrs Kemp stopped and refused to go on. 'I want to talk to Gregory,' she said. 'You promised I could.'

'He might have stayed in town last night,' Melissa said. 'Gina can go down and check if he's back.'

Gina hurried away obediently, and Mrs Kemp remained motionless, her jaw set and her eyes narrowed as she watched Gina's progress down the path to the chalet. Gina disappeared from sight for several moments before reappearing and coming back to where they waited.

'He didn't come back last night, and rang the housekeeper this morning to say he would be staying in town until this evening,' Gina reported.

'He's trying to avoid me,' Mrs Kemp said petulantly, and moved on with quick, angry steps.

They returned to the villa, and Mrs Kemp stretched out on her bed and closed her eyes. Gina signalled to Melissa to leave the room, and followed quietly, locking the door.

'She'll probably sleep until lunchtime,' Gina said. 'The rest will do her good. If there's anything you want to do, now would be a good time to do it. I'll be here in case she calls.'

'I'll be in my room,' Melissa decided. 'I need to check over my clothes. Call me if you should need me.'

She was pensive as she attended to her own chores, her thoughts giving her no rest. When she recalled the previous evening, it seemed like a dream, and Jasmine's scream as she fell into the trap had shattered all sense of reality.

So there was active smuggling in the area! Melissa recalled the darkened boat that had crossed the bay when she was on the yacht with Russell and the professor. But who was involved in such criminal activity? She could not believe that Russell was, or Jasmine. And would Christopher Kemp dabble in such a shady business? His family were reputed to be millionaires! And Gregory Lombard was an established writer who should have sufficient intelligence to keep away from anything so unsavoury.

Thinking about it did not help to clear the situation, and Melissa gave up in the end. When it was time for lunch, she collected Mrs Kemp's tray from the kitchen and took it up to the bedroom. Gina was inside, talking with the patient, and Melissa left them alone, believing that Mrs Kemp would be better off without a comparative stranger watching her.

She went down to the dining room for lunch, and was surprised to find

Christopher seated at the long table. He greeted her affably, and she regarded him with suspicion because he was always so nasty towards her. He laughed and shook his head.

'You should just see your face,' he remarked. 'You don't know that I have another side to my nature, do you? I can be quite friendly when I want to be.'

'So what have I done to warrant such a change?' Melissa countered. 'You weren't friendly at breakfast.'

'I can see that you take your job very seriously, and really want to help my mother, so I'll treat you with more respect. I'd like to take you out this evening for a trip in my boat. I know you're seeing Russell Vinson in your free time, but he won't be available tonight — I saw him getting on the steamer this morning to go to the mainland, and there's no boat back until tomorrow.'

Melissa's expression did not change at the news, but a pang stabbed through her because she had been so looking forward to seeing Russell again. So he had gone to the mainland! She was wondering if it had anything to do with the trouble last night when she became aware that Christopher was watching her closely, and controlled her expression.

'Well?' he asked. 'Would you like a trip across the bay as the sun goes down? You might not get another chance at it. The professor's yacht doesn't up-anchor from one week to another, so it's down to me to take you.'

'I don't know how Mrs Kemp will be later,' Melissa said, shaking her head. 'I might not be able to get away.'

'Gina's been coping alone for weeks; she can manage for another night. I'll drive you into town around seven, and we'll cast off in time to see the sunset from the best possible position in the bay.'

Melissa considered, and it was the thought that she might be able to discover if he was involved in anything nefarious that decided her to accept his invitation. 'All right,' she said. 'I'll tell Gina where and who I'm going with.'

'So you don't really trust me!' He laughed. 'Are you afraid you might disappear like my brother Kenneth did seven years ago?'

'No! But Gina will need to know where I'll be.'

'Very well. I'll be out front with my car at seven.' He got up and left the room.

Melissa wondered what she had let herself in for. But she did not suspect Christopher of being involved in smuggling, and accepted that he was genuinely trying to be friendly. However, she was filled with anticipation when she went out to the terrace just before seven and found him waiting impatiently for her.

'I began to think you'd changed your mind,' he commented. 'Come on — I'm sure you'll enjoy this. And I like night cruising.'

Melissa was mainly silent on the drive to town, recalling the previous evening when Russell had taken her there. Then she had been filled with anticipation; but now she felt depressed, and realised it was because Russell was away and she could not see him. 'Did you hear about the animal trap that was dug in the path leading up to the monastery last night?' she asked.

'Animal trap?' He glanced at her, his dark eyes expressionless. 'Yes, I gave permission for it to be dug.'

'*You* did?' Melissa was aghast. 'What on earth for?'

'Why would an animal trap be dug if not to catch an animal?'

'Jasmine Pollard fell into it last night as she was returning from town. It's a wonder she wasn't injured.'

'Don't tell me the trap was dug in the path itself!'

'Of course it was! How do you suppose Jasmine fell into it? She wouldn't leave the path after dark. Why did you give permission for the trap to be dug?

183

And, more to the point — who dug it?'

'There's a small zoo on the next property along the coast. One of their wolves escaped a couple of days ago, and it was spotted on our property. They wanted to trap it rather than shoot it, so I gave them permission, but I didn't think they'd be so stupid as to dig a pit in a public footpath. I'll sort it out tomorrow.' He laughed. 'So flighty Miss Pollard fell into it, did she? I wish I'd seen it.'

Melissa gazed at him in amazement, but his explanation quelled a number of clamouring questions jumbled in her brain. She had begun to think that murder would probably be committed next, but the tension drained out of her at his reasonable explanation, and she sighed deeply.

They left the car on the quay and crossed to a very large and powerful cabin cruiser. It was a seagoing vessel, and Melissa wondered if it was involved in local smuggling. Christopher seemed eager now, and there a boyish note in his tone as he talked about the craft. She stood in the cockpit and tried to keep out of his way as he performed a series of checks and then switched on the ignition. He cast off, and there was a tremendous roar as he ran up the engine to full power. The vessel leapt forward like an impatient greyhound, its sharp bows slicing through the calm water like a hot knife cutting butter.

Melissa sat down on a cushioned seat in the stern. She was unable to see much ahead because a large bow wave curled away on either side, tossing spray back at them, and a long white furrow astern showed turbulently when she looked over her shoulder. They sped south, and roared across the bay where the professor's yacht was at anchor. Christopher steered straight at the moored craft, turning aside at the last moment, and rocked it violently with his wash.

The sun was low on the horizon, almost out of sight below it, as they headed out into the misty strait.

Christopher sat nonchalantly on his seat, his immobile face illuminated by a dull green light emanating from the control panel in front of him. He looked around at Melissa as they left the shelter of the bay, and the deck under her feet began lifting and falling gently as the boat met the swell of the open sea.

'As soon as we're in clear water, I'll show you around the boat,' he called. 'It's much larger below than it looks from here.'

Melissa twisted in her seat and looked at her surroundings. She was already regretting her decision to accompany him, being only too aware that she was now completely at his mercy if he had any intention of harming her. Perhaps he was one of the local smugglers. If he was, then she could be in serious trouble, and she should have considered the possibility before going with him. The sun was almost gone now, just a small segment showing above the horizon. Stars were already shining remotely in the dark velvet sky, and the full moon in the east was casting a silver pathway from the side of the boat out to the horizon.

The craft raced on at top speed and, despite her fears, Melissa found it exhilarating to stand gripping a rail and looking forward over the uplifted bows. If only Russell was here instead of Christopher! As the thought crossed her mind, she realised that subconsciously she was accepting Russell into her life and her heart, despite her feeble attempts to remain impervious to his charms.

For perhaps an hour they sped through the night, leaving a creamy wake astern to mark their passing. Then without warning, the engine cut out. They lost speed immediately and a heavy silence closed in around them. Melissa turned her attention to Christopher and saw him operating a lever on the instrument panel. When he glanced up at her, he had a puzzled expression on his face.

'What's the trouble?' she asked.

'A bit of dirt in the feed pipe, I expect. It may clear itself in a moment.'

Almost immediately the engine burst into life again, ran sweetly for two minutes, and then died quickly. Melissa tensed and moved away from him. 'Are we in danger?' she asked, stifling an involuntary shudder as she glanced around at the shadowed sea.

'No, nothing like that. I'll have to check the pipes, and I don't need you under my feet. We're cramped for space and I have to take up a couple of deck plates. I'll show you into a cabin where you'll be comfortable. I'll be about twenty minutes sorting this out, but don't worry — this has happened before, and I know what's wrong and can put it right.'

Melissa followed him down a narrow companionway. He took her into the big forward cabin and switched on a light. 'Make yourself at home,' he invited. 'I'd better hurry back on deck. Help yourself to a drink.' He paused

188

and subjected her to a close scrutiny. 'You're looking a bit pale. Are you a poor sailor, or just frightened of me?'

'Why should I be afraid of you?' she countered, meeting his gaze without flinching. 'Perhaps I'm not a very good sailor.'

'We're rolling a bit, but it'll be better when I've got the engine going again. Just relax.' He smiled crookedly. 'If you do suspect my motives, then bolt the door when I leave. It'll be all right by me.'

Melissa shrugged, entered the cabin and closed the door. She sat down on an upholstered seat and tried to relax, wondering if the breakdown was genuine or had in some way been contrived. She sat very still, listening intently but hearing nothing. The silence seemed ominous, and she wondered if Christopher had returned to the cockpit to check the engine or was waiting outside the cabin door, steeling himself for the ruthless chore of getting rid of her. Was this how his brother Kenneth had disappeared?

She knew she could not prevent her nerves and imagination from working against her, and as the minutes passed she began to fear that she would never again set foot on land. She paced the small cabin, waiting and wondering for what seemed an eternity, until the engine roared, splitting the deathly silence with its sweet sound. It spluttered and then died.

Melissa found the strain unbearable as she paced to and fro. There were two portholes at the bows, almost opposite each other, and she crossed to one and peered through it, hoping to spot the twinkling lights of the island. But blank darkness baffled her eyes and she turned to the other porthole, looked out, and got the shock of her life.

They were not alone out here in the night. A large craft without lights was rising and falling on the swell just yards away. She saw dark, anonymous figures on the deck of the ghostly craft, and then a splash as they heaved a long cylindrical object into the water with a line attached to it. Christopher began hauling in the slack. He moved aft out of Melissa's line of sight, and moments later the engine started and ran without hesitation. The other craft moved quickly away.

Melissa sat down again, wondering what was going on. Had Christopher brought her along this evening as a cover for some nefarious business? The boat suddenly shuddered and a dull thud sounded. It seemed to come from directly below her feet, as if something had grated against the keel. Then she heard the sound of Christopher's feet in the companionway outside.

She closed her eyes, feigning sleep, and wondered, as she heard the cabin door opening, if they would be returning to port now — or was Christopher coming to deal with her?

8

Melissa started nervously when Christopher touched her shoulder. She sat up, pretending she didn't know where she was, and looked at his face. He was smiling. She looked around as if suddenly recalling her whereabouts.

'I'm sorry! I must have fallen asleep,' she said. 'I'm not very good company, am I?'

'That's all right.' Relief sounded in his voice. 'I've fixed the engine. It's always a difficult job to do out here. We can go back to the harbour now. And I'm the one who should be sorry. After your long day, I should have had more sense than to bring you out here. Come up to the cockpit. The fresh air will blow away your sleepiness. You can steer us back to the harbour, if you like.'

Melissa followed him up to the deck

and looked around quickly for signs of the craft that had been alongside them, but there was nothing but the empty, shadowed sea. She declined Christopher's invitation to pilot the craft and sat in the stern, watching him intently, wondering if he meant to throw her overboard to get rid of her. But her mind was still trying to puzzle out what had happened when the two boats had met.

It was obvious now that the engine failure had been contrived, and fortunately not for the reason she had at first imagined. Christopher had deliberately stopped for the rendezvous with that unknown craft, and something had been transferred from one boat to the other. She could see no trace of anything at all, and thought there should be water on the deck if something had been dragged out of the sea. The object that had been transferred had been large enough to make the splash she had heard from inside the cabin, and there was not space enough for a bulky object to be concealed on the boat.

But the mysterious thud she had heard seemed to have come from the keel! What could have caused that? She tossed her thoughts around and tried to find a logical answer. Soon she spotted the lights of the harbour ahead; they were easing in towards the quay, and she still had not come up with a plausible explanation for what had happened.

'We've been out for a few hours,' Christopher said as he cut the engine. They glided in the last few yards. 'It was a good run, apart from that little spot of trouble. I'm sorry about that. I'll get the marine engineer to run his rule over the engine before putting out again. I hope you enjoyed the trip. Will you come out again?'

'I'd love to,' she lied, and was filled with a great sense of relief as he jumped ashore with a line.

He tied up, then came back aboard to lock up. As he bent over the companion-way, Melissa, looking around the quayside, saw several dark figures suddenly appear and converge on the boat. Two men leapt down on to the deck, and Melissa called out to Christopher. He came quickly to her side in the cockpit, and she saw his face harden in the moonlight.

'Who are you and what do you want?' he demanded in a husky tone.

'Police and customs officers,' the foremost man replied. 'Just stay where you are.'

'What the devil is going on?' Belligerence sounded in Christopher's tone, and his grip on Melissa's arm tightened convulsively.

'We're carrying out a routine check on every vessel entering the harbour tonight,' was the steady reply. 'We need to search your boat, Mr Kemp.'

Christopher did not hesitate, and when he spoke his voice was smooth and normal. 'Just as you wish. You startled me, jumping from out of nowhere like that. I'll unlock the boat again.'

Four men came aboard, tilting the craft with their combined weight.

Melissa stood silent and motionless with Christopher at her side while the men began their search. A Greek uniformed policeman stood with them in the cockpit, and they could hear sounds of the search taking place below.

'Am I suspected of smuggling?' Christopher asked the policeman.

'Not at all, Mr Kemp. This is just routine. We do make these snap checks from time to time. We cannot make any exceptions to the order. It would be more than our jobs are worth to overlook your boat.'

'I see! Well, I suppose you people have your duty to do.' There was a grudging note in Christopher's voice, and Melissa studied his profile while he was gazing at the quayside. He was obviously on edge, and suddenly she thought she knew why he was concerned. That strange shudder and grating sound, as if a heavy metal object had banged against the keel . . . Melissa's eyes narrowed as she considered. Had contraband been placed in a metal container and attached to the keel by some kind of magnet? She caught her breath as the thought played through her mind. If that was the answer, then it was an ingenious method of evading customs.

She stood trembling with excitement until the search was over. The men left quickly, the policeman murmuring his thanks and apologies for delaying them. Christopher locked up again and then helped Melissa ashore, and she was certain that he was most relieved. He was smiling as they got into his car and started back along the coast road to the villa. 'Do customs officers often search the ships coming in and out of the harbour?' she asked, aware that she should show some interest in what had happened.

'Now and again. We're very close to international waters, and I suspect that a lot of smuggling does go on. In fact, I know some islanders who have made a business of smuggling for centuries. It's a trade that's been handed down from father to son for centuries.' He laughed harshly. 'I wonder what they were looking for on my boat! Whatever it is, they wouldn't find a thing if they searched for a month.'

By the time they reached the villa, Melissa was impatient to see Russell, to tell him of her suspicions before Christopher had the opportunity to remove the burden fastened to the keel of his boat. As they alighted from the car, Christopher glanced at his watch.

'You've had a busy day today,' he declared, 'so I suppose you're ready for bed. It's almost midnight, but I'm not an early bird. I think I'll visit Gregory, have a couple of drinks with him and a game of chess. I'll see you tomorrow — and don't forget that you take up your nursing duties in the morning.'

'I won't forget. And thank you for the trip; I enjoyed it. Goodnight.' Melissa turned and crossed to the terrace, losing herself in the shadows by the wall of the villa as Christopher turned the car and drove off at top speed.

She paused in the darkness and watched the tail-lights of the car disappearing along the twisty road, her eyes narrowed and filled with conjecture. She fancied that she had discovered an important point about the shady dealings that were going on, and although she only suspected that Russell was connected to the police, she had to get the information to him as soon as possible.

Her anticipation increased as she considered, and she went onto the front terrace and moved to the low wall, peering out at the moored yacht. But it was in partial darkness — the moon had changed its position — and she drew a deep breath because she knew she had to go down to the beach and make her way out to the vessel.

Footsteps suddenly sounded somewhere close by, and Melissa froze and peered into the shadows. The next instant she saw Andrea Kemp emerging from the villa. She paused on the terrace, silhouetted by the light coming out behind her, then closed the door and hurried around to the side terrace. A moment later Melissa heard a car door slam, and saw the sweep of headlights as Andrea drove away.

Trying to bolster her faltering nerve, Melissa went into the house. She looked in the kitchen, but there was no sign of Gina. She then went silently into her room, put on her bathing suit under her dress, and left the villa once more. For some moments she stood in the shadows around the steps leading to the beach path, her pulse racing as she considered the risk she was taking. She was afraid of going along that dark path under the trees, but there was nothing else for it, and she clenched her hands and started down the steps, her sandals making no sound at all.

She glanced around nervously as she started slowly along the path. When heard voices somewhere ahead, she flitted to one side and dropped lightly into the undergrowth, lying motionless and afraid, until she recognised Gina's voice. She raised herself slightly and caught a glimpse of two figures, but she could not understand what was being said in Greek. As soon as the pair had gone, she slipped out of cover and continued slowly to the beach.

The moon had sailed across the sky, leaving the bay in partial darkness. Melissa halted on the beach and looked around. Her heart was pounding and her nerves felt almost at breaking point. When she considered what she had to do, she almost lost her determination. But she could not wait until morning to see Russell, because Christopher had gone to see Gregory Lombard and would have reported the safe arrival of the latest consignment of contraband, which would be removed from the keel of the boat before any police action could be taken.

She took off her dress and stood in the chill breeze in her swimsuit, aware that her pale skin would show up clearly to any eyes watching the beach. She could not see the yacht until she crouched and put its deck and mast into silhouette. The knowledge that she had to warn Russell of the latest developments made her squirm, but she waded into the water up to her waist and took a long, quivering breath. For another moment she paused; the slightest unnatural noise would have sent her scurrying back to the beach and the comparative safety of the villa. But nothing disturbed her, and she slid forward into the bay and breast-stroked out towards the silent, darkened craft.

After a few yards her fears began to recede. She could not be seen in the shadows. She breathed deeply and regularly, her gaze fixed on the boat. It did not appear to be getting any closer, and the water seemed surprising cold now. But she struck out steadily, and soon found herself under the shadow of the yacht.

She clambered into the dinghy, moored beside the parent ship, and then swung herself to the deck of the yacht. As she straightened, a figure arose from cover and confronted her, and she saw the waning moonlight glinting on a gun.

'Melissa!' It was Russell confronting her, and she sighed in relief. His voice was filled with shock as she stared at her in disbelief. 'What on earth has brought you out here?'

'I'll tell you as soon as I regain my breath,' she gasped.

'Come down to the cabin and I'll get you a towel.' He took her arm. 'I daren't show a light up here, so be careful.'

He led the way below the deck and into a cabin, then closed the deadlights before switching on a light. The professor was asleep on a bunk, but opened his eyes as soon as the darkness was dispelled. He gazed in amazement at Melissa, who was dripping water all over the floor.

Russell handed her a large towel and she wrapped herself in it. His face was intent as he stared at her. 'We heard by radio that you went out on Christopher's boat,' he said sharply. 'You were taking a big chance after the warning you received.'

'I thought I could learn something that would help you,' she said.

The professor smiled. 'And you have, eh? I'm sure you wouldn't have swum out here at this time of night if it wasn't a matter of the utmost importance.'

'You're right.' Melissa hugged herself inside the towel, shivering. She quickly explained what had happened during her trip with Christopher; and when she described the meeting with the unknown boat, both Russell and the professor looked excited. Then she told them her theory about contraband being fixed to the keel, probably by a magnet, and the professor could remain silent no longer.

'That could be it!' he said instantly. 'By heaven, Russell, we could get them now. No wonder they've never been worried by the searches that have been made. They must have an electromagnet attached to the keel. The contraband is never on the boat, it's always underneath it. They've been laughing at us. Get on the radio, Russell, and report it to headquarters.'

'We've been slowly closing in on them,' Russell agreed. 'But attaching the contraband to the keel must be the reason there's been so much underwater activity in the bay.'

'You must hurry!' Melissa gasped. 'I swam out here tonight because the contraband is still attached to Christopher's keel, and you need to get it before he can remove it. When we got back to harbour, Christopher brought me back to the villa and then went to see Gregory Lombard. I might be wrong, but they could be on their way right now to remove the evidence.' She paused and gazed at the two intent men. 'Unless, of course, you're not policemen, as I suspect, but smugglers also.'

Russell laughed. 'I've always had a doubt about the professor,' he said. 'But as you know so much about our activities now, I'd better introduce us properly before you get any more strange ideas. The professor is a police superintendent, and I'm a detective inspector. We're working with Europol — narcotics — and I hope you'll keep this to yourself, Melissa. You've given us the breakthrough we've been hoping for, and if you'll excuse me for a moment, I'll get in touch with the Greek police and start the ball rolling.' He smiled at her and left the cabin.

'You're a remarkable woman, Miss Harley!' the professor said. 'You certainly have more than your share of cold nerve. But I'm afraid you're getting rather too deeply involved in our business. I must repeat the warning I gave you. Leave your position here and return to England as soon as possible.'

'But I'm taking up my nursing duties with Mrs Kemp tomorrow!' Melissa told him about Christopher's information from his father. 'They must have overcome their suspicions about me and realised that I'm nothing more than an ordinary nurse.'

'You'll never be just that,' he responded. 'But I'll have you watched after this, and you must take precautions. Never go off anywhere alone, and be careful of the company you keep.'

She nodded. 'What happens when your case is finished?'

'We'll move on to another one. I'm afraid you may be out of a job when we make our arrests. The Kemps will go to prison, and Mrs Kemp will have to go into a care home.'

'Are they all involved then?'

'As far as I know,' he replied.

Russell returned, looking satisfied. 'It's all being taken care of,' he announced. 'I'd better take Melissa back to the villa — and this time, my dear, you'd better go straight to bed. No more wandering around. I think the situation will heat up quickly now, and if you act suspiciously around the villa then you might invite trouble.'

'After tonight I won't have spare time

for anything beyond my nursing duties,' she replied.

Russell led the way up to the deck, and turned to her in the shadows, placing his hand on her bare shoulders. She saw his teeth gleaming and knew he was smiling, but his words saddened her. 'I'll be extremely sorry when this case comes to an end,' he said softly.

'Because it means you'll have to leave the island for another case.' She nodded. 'The professor told me. And I'll be sorry to see you go, Russell.'

'You'll probably be out of a job as well,' he mused. 'Will you return to London?'

'I expect so.' Her tone was low.

'Whatever you do, keep in touch with me,' he said huskily, and his hands tightened on her slim shoulders.

'I'll give you my home address.' She did not want to think of the future. So much had happened since her arrival that she was reluctant to allow her mind to contemplate the time when it might all be over with — all too soon.

'I'll be spending a lot of time in London afterwards,' Russell said. 'I was loaned to Interpol just for this case. I'll see you again, Melissa.' He paused, and then added, 'That's if you'd like to see me again.'

'I should like to very much.' She spoke boldly, for she wanted him to know that she regarded him as someone special.

He sighed and allowed his hands to slip from her shoulders. 'A lot will happen before this is finished, and I need to make sure nothing bad happens to you. We're dealing with quite ruthless men. Please be careful, Melissa.'

'I will,' she promised. 'I won't give them any cause to suspect me. Now I'd better be getting back to the villa before I'm missed.'

He helped her into the dinghy, cast off, and took up the oars. She sat in the stern, facing him as he rowed lustily. The stars seemed brighter than she had ever seen them before, and a wave of emotion uplifted her mind. But her happiness was tinged with sorrow, for here she was in a lover's paradise, yet there was a sense of worry and fear in the background that tainted the romance that seemed to have blossomed between herself and Russell.

Tiny waves lapped against the stem of the dinghy as it moved slowly between yacht and shore, the slight sounds like the caresses of a beaming mother nature, smiling upon their pleasure. Melissa breathed deeply, taking in impressions of the night that would remain with her for the rest of her life.

'This is all too much like a dream,' she said in a soft tone, half-afraid to break the silence for fear of losing the spell that seemed to grip her. 'My life has changed completely since arriving here, and it's all been so sudden.'

'Life is like that,' Russell said. 'You never know what's waiting around the corner. Personally, my job has prevented me from looking ahead. Duty is a hard mistress.'

Melissa mentally agreed, and fervently hoped that this time duty would relent a little and give them a chance to discover if there was any possibility of a future for them together. Intuition was hinting that he would become very important to her.

A swirl in the water alongside the boat distracted her from her fast-moving thoughts. At first she thought it was one of the oars skimming through the flat surface of the sea, but this was close in. And as she peered down at the dark surface of the water, she saw a disturbance right at the side of the dinghy: a breaking of the surface by a large, shiny black object. Before she could shout a warning, two hands grasped the side of the boat, and a frogman's head and shoulders reared up out of the depths like a sea monster intent on its prey.

Melissa stared at the intruder in disbelief. Time seemed to freeze as shock bolted through her. Then she opened her mouth to cry out to warn

Russell, who was rowing steadily for the shore. She was constricted by fear; but even so, she managed to cry out sharply. Before Russell could react, however, the boat was tipped very quickly and violently. The next instant it was capsized, and Melissa only had time to gasp for air before she hit the water and went plunging down into the dark depths, taking with her a vision of Russell lunging out of his seat toward her, trying to grasp her. But she could not reach his outstretched hands, and they separated and went down in a flurry of panicky movements.

Melissa fought the fear that clawed inside her, and kicked her way back to the surface. She had closed her eyes instinctively as she entered the water, but now opened them and looked around as her head bobbed above the surface. The sea was shadowed and seemed filled with hostility. The dinghy was to her left and floating upside down. They were not so far from the shore. But there was no sign of Russell or the sinister figure of the frogman.

She fought down her horror as she looked around for Russell. Her heart was pounding, her nerves taut and finely stretched almost to breaking point. Shock had followed shock so quickly since her arrival on the island. All the talk of the danger she was in did not really impress itself on her, because deep down she had felt that nothing untoward could possibly happen to her.

She dashed water from her eyes, and saw a patch of disturbed water nearby. Two heads broke the surface simultaneously, and one belonged to the frogman. Their arms thrashed, turning the smooth surface into a broiling vortex. Melissa cringed when she saw the glitter of starlight on a long blade in the frogman's hand. Then both heads sank beneath the surface again, and a stab of fear shot through her.

She dived, but could not see either man. Rising to the surface again, she looked around desperately, treading water, her arms working steadily as she looked around. Then she felt a body brush against her legs, and instantly darted sideways to avoid further contact. The sight of the long knife had terrified her; she could almost feel it slicing through her tender flesh.

The two heads broke the surface again, very close together and almost within an arm's length of Melissa. She saw Russell's face, pale in the moonlight. He was struggling furiously, with both hands around the wrist of the hand holding the knife, trying the shake the weapon loose from the frogman's grasp.

She surged forward, moving around to get behind the frogman, and ignoring Russell's rasping shout to make for the safety of the shore. She grappled with her opponent, her hands slipping uselessly on the wet rubber of his suit; but then she caught hold of his goggles and exerted pressure, lifting her knees to the small of his back and throwing her weight backwards, gasping for air as she went under the surface again.

The frogman had to go with her, and he yelled in Greek as he went under. Russell did not let go of him, and they kicked in the water until they rose once more to the surface. They were like two sharks fighting for the same prey, and Melissa had no time to feel scared. She kept her grip on the frogman's head, filled with the thought that if he escaped he would use his knife on her. But Russell maintained his hold and they continued to thrash around.

Melissa concentrated on trying to wrench the man's mouthpiece away to cut off his air supply. He was in his element while he could get air, and they were at a disadvantage. Her clawing fingers were desperate. The frogman was quick to realise his danger, and his sense of surprise had already been lost. He dropped his knife and lashed out with his hands and feet. He was suddenly on the defensive, trying desperately to get clear. When Melissa's feet touched the seabed, she braced her feet against it and then lunged away from the frogman, both hands in a death grip on his mouthpiece. She felt it pull away from him, and knew fierce exultation as she shot up to the surface with it still in her hands. Russell and the frogman went with her, and when their heads broke the surface they all gasped for air.

Russell had worked his way behind the man and took him in a stranglehold. Melissa closed in, pulling on the man's airlines, and the frogman was quickly towed to the beach. When their feet touched bottom and they could stand up, the frogman renewed his resistance. Melissa clung to her hold while Russell tried to land a knock-out blow. She heard the sharp crack of Russell's knuckles against the mysterious attacker's jaw, and the next instant the man was crumpling in the shallows.

They were breathing heavily as they dragged the body ashore onto firm sand. Melissa dropped to the beach and gasped for breath as shock set in. She was trembling uncontrollably, filled with a host of strange emotions. She looked up to see Russell kneeling beside the unconscious frogman; he was peering into the man's dark face.

'Do you know him?' she asked.

'It's Gina's boyfriend Nick,' Russell replied.

Melissa drew a quick breath. 'He was taking Gina back to the villa when I was on the path coming down to the yacht to talk to you.'

'Then he must have seen someone at the villa who warned him. Perhaps you've already been missed from your room, Melissa!'

'I told you, Christopher left as soon as he dropped me off. He said he was going to Gregory Lombard's chalet.'

'He could have been lying.' Russell was breathing heavily. 'But now we have a little more to work on. Nick is mixed up in this business, that we do know, and he'll have to explain how and why.'

'What are you going do with him?'

'Keep him under arrest for a spell, at least until he talks.' Russell glanced around. The dinghy was drifting in towards the shore, bottom up. 'Can you bring the dinghy to the beach?' he asked.

Melissa got up without hesitation, waded into the sea, and then struck out for the little craft. She had no difficulty towing it in, and Russell came to her side when she reached the shallows, quickly righting the boat and bringing its anchor to bury it in the sand. The oars were still in place in the rowlocks.

'Thank you for what you've done,' Russell said. 'I want you to get back to the villa now, as quickly as you can, and act as if nothing has happened since you left Christopher. Don't tell Gina about Nick.'

'But she's already terribly worried about him! She's been crying on and off all day.'

'I'm sorry about that, but that's the way it has to be. I'll come and see you tomorrow as soon as I can. If I can't make it during the day, then it'll be in the evening.' He kissed her lips. 'Now please go, Melissa.'

She opened her mouth to protest but he silenced her with another kiss. She turned and left the beach, pausing when she reached the pines. Looking back, she saw Russell seated in the stern of the dinghy while Nick rowed it out to the yacht. She turned away, suddenly feeling utterly weary. She located her dress and put it on, then started through the shadows towards the villa, filled with a mixture of fear and relief.

9

When Melissa awakened the next morning, she lay motionless for several moments, running through everything that had occurred the evening before. She could not believe how she had been so caught up in those dramatic events. All she had wanted to do was take care of her patient, but she had been attracted to Russell almost against her will, and sensed that the loss of pride she'd suffered when her unhappy relationship in England had ended might have made her vulnerable to him. She lingered on her thoughts of him, and realised that there was more to the situation than mere attraction. She had felt a definite surge of deeper feelings the moment they met on the island boat.

She arose quickly as her mind veered into dangerous waters, stifling her musings by focusing instead on her nursing duties. She prepared for the day's routine, but her resolution faltered badly when she met up with Gina in the kitchen. She had red-rimmed eyes and looked as if she had not slept a wink during the night.

'Gina, are you all right?' Melissa asked.

'I'm worried about Nick,' replied Gina in a quivering tone. 'I was supposed to see him when I went off duty last night, but he never turned up, and I waited for over an hour before I went home. He's caught up in some bad business and won't, or can't, get out of it. I gave him a warning that I would leave him if he didn't do the right thing, so I suppose he's decided to let me go in favour of his friends.'

'I'm so sorry,' Melissa said. 'Isn't there anything you can do?'

Gina shook her head, and tears ran down her cheeks.

'I want to take Mrs Kemp out this morning,' Melissa changed the subject abruptly. 'We'll go along the shore, cut inland past Gregory's chalet, and walk through the fields before coming back. Mrs Kemp will feel much better for plenty of exercise.'

'I agree, but we're not supposed to take her out unless Nick is with us,' Gina reminded her.

'I think we can manage without Nick's help. Let's get her up, give her a good breakfast, and then we'll be on our way.'

Gina's expression brightened immediately. 'I'll get her up and see what kind of mood she's in while you see to her breakfast. Let's get out early and give her a good time.'

Their patient was in a pleasant mood when they led her from the house and set off through the pines to the beach. But when they reached the shore, Mrs Kemp refused to go any further. 'I don't want to go on the beach,' she said petulantly. 'I want to go up to the monastery first and see the girls. We can come back the other way and go to the cliffs above the bay. I like the view from there, and I might see my Kenny coming home from his trip. He's been gone such a long time now.'

They retraced their steps and followed the path up through the trees to the ruins. There was no sign of Russell, Melissa noted, and the professor was not there. Jasmine greeted them, and Mrs Kemp got down on her hands and knees beside her and began to grub in the dust. Gina knelt beside their charge while Melissa looked down over the stretch of pines to the bay, spotting the yacht moored there. It looked deserted, and she wondered what had happened during the night. She watched Gina with Mrs Kemp and her heart went out to her, aware as she was that Nick was in police custody and facing trouble.

Mrs Kemp soon tired of her activity, and they left the ruins and followed the inner path down to the shore, eventually reaching the low cliffs overlooking the bay at a point to the left of Gregory Lombard's chalet. Mrs Kemp paused to enjoy the scene. Gina was in close attendance, her right hand under Mrs Kemp's left elbow. Melissa stood behind Mrs Kemp.

Sunlight glinted on the smooth surface of the bay. The smell of the pines was heavy in the warm air. Directly below where they were standing, the water was close up against the low cliffs, and a scattering of small rocks were showing their tops just above the water. Melissa shifted her gaze to the left, looking at Gregory's chalet. It looked deserted, and Melissa wondered what had occurred in the night after she had left Russell.

At that moment, Gina uttered a loud cry. Melissa dragged her thoughts back to her patient and gasped in horror when she saw Gina sprawling on the grass and Mrs Kemp in the act of jumping off the cliff into the sea. For a heart-stopping moment, Melissa was frozen in shock; then she stepped forward a pace to the edge of the cliff and saw Mrs Kemp entering the water, barely missing a jagged rock. As her patient disappeared below the surface of the bay, Melissa drew a deep breath, picked a spot that seemed bare of rocks, and hurled herself off the cliff.

She entered the water cleanly, her eyes open, and caught a glimpse of Mrs Kemp's blue dress. She kicked powerfully and reached out with grasping fingers. Mrs Kemp was not struggling. Her eyes were closed, her hands limp at her sides, and her mouth was closed as if she was holding her breath. Melissa caught hold of her right shoulder and kicked for the surface, dragging the inert woman with her. When she broke the surface, she gasped for breath and looked around. The sea was calm. She swung Mrs Kemp around to get behind her, pushed her left arm over the woman's shoulder, and cupped her left hand under her chin. Mrs Kemp did not struggle. She seemed unconscious.

There was a small stretch of beach to Melissa's left and she made for it, towing Mrs Kemp and keeping her mouth above water. When she glanced to her left she saw Gina on the headland, walking along and keeping pace with them. Melissa swam until her feet touched sand, then stood up and grasped Mrs Kemp under the arms. As she struggled ashore with her burden, Mrs Kemp became animated and began fighting to get away, crying and screeching when she failed to break Melissa's grip.

Gina arrived, and between them they pulled Mrs Kemp onto firm sand. Melissa crouched by the woman's side and examined her. Mrs Kemp seemed none the worse for the incident. She was silent now, her eyes closed, dark lashes stark against her pale cheeks.

'That was the last thing I expected,' Gina said in a shaky voice. 'But she's been unusually quiet this morning. I was wondering what was going on in that poor brain of hers. It's when she's quiet that she does bad things.'

Melissa glanced around. She saw the roof of Gregory's chalet, half-hidden by trees, and motioned to Gina. 'Run to the chalet and tell Mr Lombard what's happened,' she said. 'We'll need help to get Mrs Kemp back to the villa.'

Gina dashed off and Melissa sat back on her heels, watching Mrs Kemp's immobile face. The woman was breathing normally. Her face had a grey pallor, but she seemed none the worse for her immersion. Then Melissa noticed that her eyelids were flickering.

'You can open your eyes now, Mrs Kemp,' she said firmly. 'I know you're only pretending.'

Mrs Kemp looked up at Melissa. There was a world of agony in her gaze, and Melissa felt so sorry for her, aware that there was little she could do to ease her anguish. 'Let's get you up on your feet and we'll return to the villa,' she suggested. 'The next time you want to go swimming, we'll make sure you're more suitably dressed, and we'll go in together. It's much more fun that way.'

'I don't like swimming,' Mrs Kemp

227

replied as Melissa helped her to her feet.

They set off along the path, and Gina appeared, followed by Gregory, who was breathless when he reached them.

'It's all right,' Melissa said. 'Thank you for coming, Gregory, but we can manage.'

'Gina said Mrs Kemp almost drowned — would have, if you hadn't gone in after her so quickly.'

'It might have looked like that to Gina,' Melissa countered, 'but the only danger was that Mrs Kemp might have hit a rock on her way into the water.'

They left him standing on the path gazing after them as they continued. Mrs Kemp gave them no more trouble. When they reached the villa, Christopher was standing at the front door, obviously waiting for them. He shook his head sadly as he regarded his mother's bedraggled state.

'Gregory rang and told me what happened,' he said tensely. 'This isn't good enough, Nurse. I don't know what my father will have to say about it when he returns. He's gone to the mainland on business, and I'm glad he can't see the state my mother's in.'

'It wasn't Melissa's fault,' Gina said, quick to defend her colleague. 'Instead of reprimanding her, you should be thanking her for saving Mrs Kemp's life. I wouldn't have been able to get her out of the water, but Melissa coped marvellously well.'

'It's not getting her out, but the opportunity you gave her to get in, that bothers me,' Christopher said sharply. 'I thought the rule was that you didn't take her out of the villa unless Nick accompanied you.'

'Nick's away at the moment,' said Gina angrily.

'Never mind that. I think you'll be out of a job, Nurse, when my father hears about this incident, so don't make any long-term plans for the future.'

Melissa looked into his gleaming eyes. They were showing grim amusement, and she stifled a sigh, aware that he would certainly play up the incident to get rid of her. They took Mrs Kemp up to her room, got her out of her wet clothes and bathed her. Mrs Kemp refused to dress in fresh clothes but insisted on getting into bed. She closed her eyes resolutely and slept, or pretended to.

'This is a bad business,' Gina said. 'Christopher will have you out of this job now, and you're doing so well with Mrs Kemp. I've never seen her looking happier. You're good for her, Melissa, and I shall tell Mr Kemp so in no uncertain terms.'

'Don't worry about it, Gina,' Melissa replied. 'I have the feeling that Mrs Kemp will have to go back into a clinic soon, and what happened this morning won't force the decision.'

'If that happens, I'll leave,' Gina said sharply. 'I won't stay if Mrs Kemp isn't here.' She sighed. 'Well, it's no use talking about it. Why don't you go for a walk? I'll stay here in case she wakes.'

Melissa shook her head. 'You can

leave me here,' she said. 'I'll keep an eye on my patient, just in case.'

'I'll take over later, then,' Gina said. 'Are you seeing Russell this evening?'

'I don't know. I'll have to wait and see if he turns up.'

The rest of the day passed slowly. Melissa sat in Mrs Kemp's room, but her patient did not move in her bed. When it was time for lunch, Melissa went down to the kitchen, collected Mrs Kemp's meal, and took it up to the bedroom. Mrs Kemp awoke, and apparently her appetite had not been affected by her unexpected immersion in the sea. After the meal she asked for two tablets, but Melissa would not give her any, and eventually Mrs Kemp went back to sleep.

The afternoon seemed over-long. Melissa found herself glancing repeat-edly at the clock to check the time, and began to think the time-piece had stopped. But the hours wore away, and at five o'clock Gina returned and Melissa went off duty.

Melissa changed for the evening, and when she was ready she looked out at the yacht from her window, wondering where Russell had been all day. She suddenly wanted very badly to see him, but quashed her feelings and went down to the kitchen for a meal, where she was accosted by Christopher.

'What are you doing this evening?' he demanded. 'Are you seeing Russell Vinson?'

'I haven't made any arrangements as such. Why do you ask?' Melissa was wondering why Christopher had not been arrested, and had already decided that she would not accompany him again, whatever his motive.

He shrugged. 'I'm just curious, that's all.'

She escaped from his presence and went up to Mrs Kemp's room for a last check on her patient. Gina was seated by the window, reading a book aloud to Mrs Kemp. She paused and looked up when Melissa came in. 'I saw Russell going up to the monastery about half an hour ago,' she said. 'If you're hoping to see him later, you'd better try and catch up with him now. He looked as if he was in a hurry.'

Melissa nodded. She left the villa and followed the path up to the monastery. As she continued, she could feel the first pangs of anticipation creeping into her breast, and by the time she reached the ruins she was breathless and had to slow her pace. It wouldn't do to let Russell see that she was running after him, especially if he was somehow involved with Jasmine.

When she saw him standing alone on a small hillock and looking around intently, her heartbeat quickened and she experienced such a rush of emotion she could barely contain it. There was no sign of the three students. She made her way past the hut and approached Russell from behind. He must have heard her footsteps on the hard ground, for he whirled before she reached him, and his rather sombre expression was changed by a gorgeous smile. His appearance was immaculate, as if he had dressed for the occasion and was hoping to see her.

'Hello!' he exclaimed, jumping off the hillock and grasping her hands. 'I was just thinking about you, wondering if I would see you this evening. I heard what happened this morning — Mrs Kemp jumped off the cliff into the sea and you dived in and got her to safety. How is she now? None the worse for her dip, I hope.'

'She seems fine, but I wouldn't be surprised if I lose my job because of it.' She told him how Christopher had reacted. 'He's been against me from the start, and he'll have a field day when Mr Kemp returns from the mainland.'

'I expect you've wondering what happened after we parted last night.' Russell slipped an arm through hers and pulled her gently away from the hut. 'We had the keel of Christopher's boat checked by a police frogman, but nothing incriminating was found. There were signs, though, that something metallic had been clamped underneath. We'll have to wait until he goes out into the strait again and then try to catch him red-handed.'

'And when he makes his next trip, I won't be going with him.' Melissa suppressed a shiver. 'What's happened to Nick? Poor Gina's been terribly upset all day, and I've felt awful, knowing what I do and being unable to tell her anything.'

'Nick is only a small fish in this business,' Russell said. 'If he sees sense and tells us what we want to know, he might come out of it unscathed, but he's been very stubborn so far. He attacked us in the dinghy, and that's a black mark against him. Anyway, from what you told us last night, I think there's a good chance of us closing this case.'

He looked into her eyes, and Melissa felt her senses being overwhelmed by his scrutiny. At the moment it did not matter to her that he might be seeing

Jasmine on the quiet. She wanted to be in his company.

'Are you free this evening?' he asked.

'Yes. Mrs Kemp is asleep in bed and Gina is standing by at the villa.'

'I was hoping we could take a walk around Lombard's place right now. I'd like to get a look inside his boat house. He has a craft similar to Christopher's, and I'm sure they're both taking an active part in the smuggling. If you come with me, my presence in the area wouldn't look as suspicious as it would if I went alone. I know I shouldn't drag you into this, but I don't want to miss a chance to see you.'

'I'll go with you,' said Melissa readily.

'I hope you won't have cause to regret that decision,' he said.

They walked down along the path that led to the road, and paused at the exposed animal trap. 'I heard they caught the wolf that escaped from the zoo,' Russell said. 'I'm glad this trap turned out to be an innocent thing; a coincidence.'

He broke off suddenly and slid his arms around Melissa, taking her by surprise; and when he kissed her without warning, she melted into his embrace and closed her eyes. But it was a perfunctory kiss with no passion in it, and his lips slid up to her ear, his breath warm on her cheek.

'There's a man along the path, hiding behind a tree, and he's watching us. I caught a sudden movement and spotted him. It's one of the islanders we suspect of being involved in the smuggling, and he and several others have become more interested in me lately. I'd like him to think that I have nothing but romance on my mind this evening.'

'Then you'd better be more passionate,' Melissa suggested.

'With pleasure!' Russell gathered her tightly in his arms and his lips closed against her mouth.

Melissa felt her legs weakening and leaned against him. Her heart thudded, and strange tingling sensations scurried through her. She could feel his heart beating powerfully against her breast, and his arms were so tight around her she was hardly able to breathe, but she strained to get even closer to him. She relaxed her grip on reality, and they were both breathless when they broke apart. Russell smiled. His bronzed forehead was beaded with perspiration and his shirt looked damp and creased.

'Do you think that looked realistic enough to a watcher?' he asked.

'I don't know about that, but it certainly felt realistic to me,' Melissa commented.

'He's gone now.' Russell slid an arm around her shoulders and they continued down the path.

The smell of the pines was tangy, filling their surroundings with an atmosphere of open air and mother nature. Melissa could see over the tops of the trees lower down the slope, and in the distance the blue sea was almost too bright to look at in the slanting rays of the sun. The professor's yacht was stark and clear, looking like a model from this height. Melissa drew a deep, shuddering breath. All her senses seemed to have taken on a special clarity that brought everything into a finer focus than normal, and she was vibrant with elation.

She stopped suddenly, and Russell glanced at her. 'Is something wrong?' he asked.

'I caught a glimpse of movement over there to the right,' she replied, smiling. 'You'd better kiss me again. That man might still be lurking around.'

Russell laughed and took her into his arms. Their contact was like sinking into a pool of liquid desire that laved Melissa's mind and made her forget everything except the man holding her. For the first time in her life she felt that she really understood the meaning of love, and hoped she would never forget the message that emerged. Russell's lips were hard and demanding at first, but then softened and caressed her mouth, his powerful body dominating hers, encouraging her to strain against him as a burgeoning passion engulfed her.

When they drew apart, Melissa was hoping the evening would never end. She would have been content if time stopped for a hundred years. She gazed at Russell, aware that if her trip to the island did nothing else, it was teaching her more about love than she had ever learned before. He held her hand as they went on, and he seemed carefree and content, although Melissa was certain he must be heavily burdened by the weight of the problems confronting him. There were so many questions she wanted to ask him, but the knowledge that danger surrounded him like a poisonous cloud was daunting. She watched him when he was not looking at her, and wondered how he endured the strain of his job.

'We're getting close to Lombard's chalet,' Russell whispered in her ear.

'What do you want to do?'

'Ideally, I'd like to take a look inside the boat house and check the boat, if it's inside. Lombard doesn't go out in it as often as Christopher, but he makes a lot of trips at night, and that in itself is suspicious. I really shouldn't drag you any deeper into this in case anything goes wrong, but I want to get to know you better, and at the moment this is the only way I can do it. If we go down to the beach, I can leave you sitting on the sand while I sneak away to the boat house. There's a wooden quay built at the water's edge, and Lombard's boat is always moored there just before he makes a trip.'

Melissa was content to let Russell lead the way, and followed him closely when he entered a screen of young trees and went rapidly down a slope that took them to the beach. She sat down on the firm sand and Russell glanced around. 'I'll have to wait until it gets darker,' he mused.

He sat down beside Melissa and put an arm around her shoulders. She leaned against him and lowered her head against his chest. When he shifted his weight slightly, they both fell backward on the sand. Melissa laughed, and Russell turned to her, sliding his arms around her. They stretched out, and when Russell kissed her, she responded ardently.

Shadows were closing in around them when Russell finally broke their embrace. Melissa glanced around, astounded by the quick passage of time. 'I'm sorry to break this up, but I must make a move,' he said. 'I won't be long.' He got to his feet, walked into nearby cover and departed, leaving Melissa feeling alone and somewhat fearful.

She sighed and tried to relax as she looked around. The professor's yacht seemed very lonely, anchored and motionless in the bay. The shore was deserted. Melissa became tense, and the euphoria of the romantic embrace fled as worry for Russell assailed her. She tried to guess what he was doing, and half-wished she had stayed by his side, as waiting for his return and not knowing what was happening was sheer torture. She lay back on the sand and closed her eyes, reliving their passionate moments and listening intently for the sound of his return; but the passing minutes dragged by agonisingly slowly, and impatience crept into her mind like a thief in the night.

The sound of seabirds calling insistently echoed across the bay. Melissa looked around but saw nothing. The smell of the pines was strong in her nostrils. A flock of small birds suddenly appeared and flew low over the surface of the calm water, feeding while the last shreds of sunlight lasted. There was an atmosphere of serenity and peace, but Melissa suffered agonies of worry, for the silence surrounding her seemed menacing and sinister. The growing shadows under the trees filled her with trepidation, for any impenetrable patch could hide a secret watcher. She could almost feel hostile eyes studying her every movement, and sensed that an observer would know the real reason for her presence.

As time passed, she began to fear that

something might have happened to Russell because he had been gone so long. She became restless, fidgeting as the pressure got to her. She drew a deep breath and decided to go in search of him, but indecision held her in its sway, and she realised that she could make the situation infinitely more difficult for him by acting precipitately. She tried to relax, but the passage of more torturous minutes shredded her patience. She jumped up and hurried into the trees to where she had last seen Russell.

She reached the side of Gregory's boathouse without seeing any sign of Russell, and she was filled with fear. Had he been caught by the smugglers? She saw the door of the boat house standing ajar, and dim yellow light was spilling out into the encircling gloom. She wondered if Russell was inside, and started forward to check.

She was almost in the open when Gregory emerged from the low building and walked towards the chalet. She dropped into cover and lay watching until he was out of sight, wracked with fearful questions. Was Gregory going out in his boat? And where was Russell?

When Gregory had disappeared from sight, Melissa slipped out of her cover and darted to the open door of the boat house, wondering if there were other men inside. But her concern for Russell outweighed all thoughts for her own safety. She peered around the edge of the door, her heart pounding, her body trembling with fear. The place looked deserted. The motor cruiser was moored to a slatted walkway and floated in shallow water. Doors at the lower end of the boat house were open, and the last of the day's sunlight was trying to hold off the shadows of approaching night.

'Russell, are you in here?' she called, but only an echo of her voice answered in the silence. Then she heard sounds outside, coming rapidly closer, and looked around like a hunted deer.

There was a stack of large oil drums to the right of the door, away from the boat; she darted around them and crouched in their cover. He heart was pounding so strongly that she feared the sound of it might be overheard.

A moment later, Gregory entered the boat house. Melissa craned forward and risked a look around her cover. She saw him carrying a long canvas-covered object. He took the item onto the boat and. stowed it in the cockpit, then departed again.

Melissa waited a moment before jumping up and running to the boat. She had to see if Russell was on board. She jumped into the cockpit and hurried below, praying there would be enough time to look around and then get clear before Gregory returned.

A closed door at the end of a short corridor cut off the forward cabin from the rest of the boat. Melissa opened it and peered into the cabin. Her heart missed a beat when she saw a man lying on a bunk. His back was towards her.

She could see that his hands were tied behind him, and a cold shiver assailed her when she recognised Russell — she identified him in the darkness by his clothes. She ran to him and discovered that he was unconscious. There was blood on his forehead. She tried to untie his hands but made little progress, as the rope was new and stiff.

She worked feverishly, hoping against hope. Then Russell began to stir. She made some progress with the knots and was beginning to feel relieved, when she heard the thump of feet in the cockpit and then a heavy thud as another large object was placed aboard. There was a momentary silence, which was suddenly broken by the powerful roar of the boat's engine. The craft rocked and began to move forward. Dying sunlight flooded through the portholes as the craft left the boat house. The roar of the engine increased tenfold. Melissa drew a shuddering breath and leaned over Russell to look out of the nearest porthole. Her spirits sank like a stone.

The shore was already dropping behind, and the craft quickly picked up speed, bows lifting and slicing through the calm water of the bay.

She trembled as she resumed her attack on the rope binding Russell's wrists. They were trapped on the boat, which would mean trouble if Gregory discovered them; but it would be even worse if she could not free Russell! Her fingers were sore, but she ignored the pain. The man she loved was in danger, and only she could help him.

10

Melissa was gripped by a sense of unreality as she struggled to untie the rope knotted around Russell's wrists. He was inert, his eyelids flickering, but she could see that he was unconscious. He groaned, and as she redoubled her efforts to free him her seething brain tried to come to grips with the situation. If Gregory came down into the cabin just to check on Russell, then she would be caught, and she dreaded to think what might follow. The fact that Russell had been attacked and bound gave her an indication of the desperation of the smugglers.

She broke a thumbnail on the stiff rope, but it seemed that the knot she was attacking gave slightly, so she renewed her efforts, head tilted on one side, wide eyes watching the door of the cabin. She could hear nothing apart from the roar of the powerful engine, and her first intimation of worse trouble to come would be the opening of the cabin door.

A sigh escaped her when the knot finally gave and she freed Russell's hands. She used her handkerchief to remove some of the blood on his forehead, and saw a large bruise where the skin had split. 'Russell!' She called his name in an undertone, although she could not be heard above the roar of the engine. 'Can you hear me? Please open your eyes and look at me.'

His eyelids flickered and he groaned. His limbs jerked and he lifted a hand to his head. When he opened his eyes fully they were vacant. He groaned again and put both hands over his face.

'Look at me, Russell,' Melissa commanded.

He jerked up as he caught the sound of her voice, and his head swivelled round. Animation filtered into his gaze, which turned to horror as he recalled recent events. 'Melissa, what are you doing here? Did they catch you, too?'

She explained what had happened. He eased himself into a sitting position.

'I admire your spirit,' he said, 'but I'd be happier if you'd gone to warn the professor instead of coming after me. He would have radioed the local police, and they could have intercepted this boat and caught Lombard red-handed.'

'I'm sorry; I didn't stop to think. I needed to find out what happened to you, so I sneaked in here and discovered you tied up, and then nothing mattered but to set you free. But Gregory came back and set out before I could do anything.'

Russell got to his feet, staggered, and sat down abruptly. Melissa dabbed at his bruise. He looked at her and shook his head. 'You've got to get off this boat before Lombard discovers you're down here,' he said.

'What would you have me do? Jump overboard?'

'It's too late for that. Give me a moment to collect my wits. Lombard struck me with something very hard.'

The air seemed oppressive in the cabin. Melissa was nervous. She fully expected Gregory to burst in any moment and overpower them. But she stifled her fears and focused on Russell. He looked a pale shadow of his normal self, and his hands were shaking. But as the moments passed, he seemed to recover from the worst effects of the blow he had received and became more animated.

'I'll go up and arrest Lombard now,' he said at length.

'Wouldn't it be better to watch him and get some evidence of his smuggling?' Melissa suggested. 'I saw him putting packages on board just before we left. I think he's going to a rendezvous with his smuggling associates.'

'You're becoming quite the detective!' Russell said, smiling faintly. He placed his hands on the bunk and leaned forward to peer through a porthole.

Melissa went to a second porthole on the other side of the cabin and looked out. She saw the distant lights of the harbour. They were a long, long way out now. The bay was behind them and they were crossing the strait itself. She went to Russell's side, and he turned and slumped down on the bunk.

'There's nothing to see out there,' he told her. 'I'll tackle Lombard. I have enough against him now to be able to put him away for a long time.'

Melissa sat by his side, holding his hand. He looked at her, forcing a smile. 'We don't seem to be able to concentrate on ourselves, do we?' he said. 'Last night we were diverted by Jasmine falling into a wolf trap, of all things, and Nick tried to drown us. Tonight the whole business has blown up in our faces. The professor warned me of the dangers of making friends with you, and at the time I disagreed with him, but now I can see my folly. I've put you in jeopardy, and I should have known better.'

'Right now I'd rather be here helping you than anywhere else.' Melissa looked around the cabin. There was nowhere to hide, and she patted Russell's hand. 'Don't worry about it,' she told him. 'If I hadn't arrived, you'd be in bad trouble now, and that doesn't bear thinking about. We can get out of this.'

'You must stay down here when I go up to arrest Lombard,' he said firmly.

Before Melissa could protest, the roar of the engine cut out suddenly, and an eerie silence enveloped the craft. Russell got to his feet.

'Take another look through that porthole,' Melissa suggested. 'This is what happened to me on Christopher's boat. He met another boat and something was transferred between them.'

Russell knelt on the bunk and peered through the porthole. He glanced at Melissa, his face showing excitement. 'There's a boat without lights coming up alongside us,' he said. 'They're smugglers, and we've got a front seat.

This is just what I need.'

Melissa remained silent. She had experienced this situation with Christopher. Russell leaned closer to the porthole.

'I can't see much,' he reported. 'There are several men on the other craft. One of them has a boathook and he's holding the two boats together with it. Ah, Lombard is going aboard the other craft.' Excitement crept into his voice. 'If I went up on deck now, I could start the engine and we could make a run for it, leaving Lombard stranded on that boat, and I'll have his packages as evidence of his guilt.'

A protest rose to Melissa's lips, but before she could speak, Russell jumped off the bunk and hurried to the cabin door. He glanced at her, his face set in determination. 'Stay down here out of danger,' he said as he departed, and Melissa caught her breath when the door closed behind him.

She went to the porthole and looked out. The other boat was alongside them now, and she saw the man with the boathook holding the two craft together. They were rocking slightly in a swell. Anonymous figures were in the stern of the other boat, and with only starlight to illuminate them, she thought she recognised one of them as Gregory, but could not be sure.

The next instant the engine roared into life, and Melissa saw sudden confusion among the men on the other boat. One of them — Gregory — jumped forward to return aboard, but Russell engaged the gears and the boat shot forward like a runaway horse. The man holding the boathook was dragged off his feet by the sudden movement and fell overboard. Gregory was caught with one foot on the other boat and one on his own, and sprawled backwards. The next instant Russell accelerated the boat swiftly into the night.

Melissa was breathless with excitement. She gulped and ran up on deck. There was no sign of the other boat now. She looked around and saw the lights of the harbour in the distance. Russell was seated at the controls. Behind him lay the four wrapped packages that Gregory had brought aboard. He was laughing with sheer excitement when Melissa joined him in the cockpit. Spray flew over the bows. Their speed was exhilarating.

'It was easy,' he shouted above the roar of the powerful engine. 'We took Lombard completely by surprise. He'll be wondering how the boat started up by itself and slipped into gear.'

'He must've seen you,' Melissa replied, grinning with sheer exuberance at their escape. She glanced back over the stern and saw nothing of the other boat. 'Will police and customs officers be waiting in the harbour when we arrive?'

'They will be, definitely, because I'm about to call headquarters and arrange for a reception committee to meet us there. Come and sit beside me and take over the steering.'

Melissa joined him and took the

wheel. He threw his arms around her and kissed her resoundingly before getting up and turning to a console. She held tightly to the wheel, pulsating with excitement at each throb of the engine. The boat was lunging forward like a greyhound in the slips. Spray smeared the windscreen in front of her. She had never felt so elated in her life. Her pulse was racing, her heart pounding, and she felt vibrant, caught up in heady excitement.

Then something struck the windscreen almost beside her head and shattered the glass. The shock of it startled her and she ducked instinctively, inadvertently jerking the wheel. The boat swung off its direct course to the harbour and half-rolled into a sharp curve. Spray flew in all directions. Russell lost his balance and sprawled across her. He fell to the floor of the cockpit and then bounded up, snatched at the wheel and brought the boat back under control.

'What happened?' he demanded, his

lips close to her right ear.

Melissa pointed to the shattered windscreen. Russell stared at it, then twisted to peer astern. He dropped into the seat beside her, took control, and spun the wheel, sending the boat into a series of zigzags. Melissa looked back and saw the mystery boat coming up fast. It was a far bigger and speedier craft than Gregory's boat. Even as she looked, there was a flash on the pursuing boat, and a second later she heard a sharp crack just to her left.

'They mean business!' Russell shouted. 'Someone is shooting at us. Get down, Melissa!'

She eased off the seat and crouched on the deck, but Russell remained where he was, controlling the boat. Fear pulsed through her mind, not for herself but for Russell. He increased their speed until they seemed to be hurtling along just above the surface of the water. But the bigger boat began to draw nearer. Russell manipulated the wheel, sending the boat into a series of tight curves, and there was no more shooting from their pursuer.

Melissa regained her seat beside Russell. The slipstream made her eyes water. She gazed at the broken windscreen and felt exhilarated despite her fear. Unreality clawed at her senses. Russell had said that life on the island was dull and mostly boring, but here they were fleeing from smugglers and being shot at.

When she looked at Russell's intent face, dimly illuminated by the green and blue lights of the control panel, she saw that he was calm and steady, his hands sure on the wheel. She looked back over the stern and was relieved to see that the following boat had given up pursuit and was heading out into the strait.

A few moments later Russell attracted her attention by pointing ahead, and she saw a brightly lit craft coming towards them from the harbour. 'That's why the smugglers are running,' he said. 'It's a customs boat coming out, and they're fast enough to catch them. Lombard's in serious trouble now.'

The radio began to chatter, and Russell motioned for Melissa to take the wheel. He got up and spoke into a microphone. The customs boat increased speed and shot past them, its wash rocking them as it headed out into the strait. Russell sat down beside Melissa, and they continued to the harbour. When they nosed into the quay, a number of men came forward and jumped aboard.

Melissa was exhausted now the excitement was over, and she felt completely drained. She slumped on her seat and remained motionless while a flurry of activity went on around her. Russell conferred with uniformed Greek police. Then the mysterious packages Gregory had brought aboard were opened, and there was excitement as the contents were examined. But it was all too much for Melissa. She began to feel uneasy, and was relieved when Russell finally turned to her.

'Lombard was carrying drugs in those packages,' he said. 'It's a pity I wasn't able to arrest him, but you were my main concern. The patrol boat that passed us should stop that other boat, and if they do we'll probably be able to put an end to this particular operation. We'll be able to leave, as the local police will take over. I've arranged for a lift back to the villa, so if you're ready we'll be on our way.'

Melissa sighed with relief. Russell put a comforting arm around her shoulders and helped her onto the stone quay. They got into the back of a police car, and Melissa leaned against Russell. He pulled her close and whispered in her ear. 'Are you all right?' he asked.

'I'm shocked,' she replied, and shivered when she looked out of the car window and saw the bay, dark and mysterious, stretching away to the horizon. She looked up into Russell's shadowed features. 'You told me there wasn't much to do around the island in the evenings, but that was an understatement if ever I heard one.'

He laughed and kissed her left temple. 'I don't want too many experiences like tonight's episode,' he said, and sighed heavily. 'I think we'll to have to stop seeing each other until this business has finished. It's much too dangerous for you, and one of our golden rules is never to involve innocent civilians.'

'I don't like the sound of that.' She leaned against him, and he kissed her forehead before moving to her lips and claiming her complete attention.

The police car dropped them at the villa, and when it had departed, Russell heaved a sigh. 'I really ought to make you go in now and ask you to forget everything that's happened,' he said quietly.

'And not see each other again,' she added.

'Would you want to see me again, after that boat trip?'

'Yes.' The word slipped out before Melissa could even consider her answer.

'Life would be so boring without you.'

He laughed and pulled her into the deep shadows at the side of the villa, and as his lips took possession of hers they both heard a furtive footstep on the nearby gravel. Russell jerked away, putting himself between Melissa and the sound. 'Who's there?' he demanded.

'Pardon my interruption.' Christopher Kemp emerged slowly from cover and came towards them. He did not stop, and went on to the terrace. 'Good night,' he called over his shoulder.

'Good night,' Russell replied, but Melissa remained silent.

Christopher paused at the corner of the villa and turned to face them. His features were just a blur in the starlight. 'Before I forget, Melissa,' he said curtly, 'my father telephoned from the mainland earlier this evening, and he was most unhappy when I gave him a report of what's happened. He's decided, in view of my mother's attempt to drown herself, to have her returned to the clinic as soon as possible. Consequently, you will be out of a job. I'm sorry to impart such bad news, but I did warn you that there was no future here for you.'

He disappeared around the corner and Melissa stood as if turned to stone, her thoughts stilled. She felt as if she were standing on the brink of a precipice. Shock froze her, and she barely felt Russell's hand on her arm.

'I'm so sorry,' he said quietly. 'You had such high hopes for Mrs Kemp. But Louis Kemp is a good man, and he might change his mind when he returns.'

'If Mrs Kemp would be better off in a clinic, then I welcome his decision,' Melissa said slowly. 'I feel so sorry for her. She's the loser in this business. She lost her son years ago, and her quality of life vanished with her peace of mind. I do wish I could have done more to help her.'

'Sleep on this tonight, and in the morning you'll be able to consider it with a clearer mind.'

'I'm too wound up to sleep,' she said slowly. 'Are you making a round of the monastery now? If you are, I'd like to accompany you. I need to come down from the high spot we hit on Gregory's boat.'

'You're a glutton for punishment!' Russell considered for a moment, then nodded. 'All right, I'll take you along — against my better judgement.'

Melissa slipped an arm through his as they walked along the path that led up to the monastery. The shadows seemed darker than before and she pressed closer to Russell, fearing that her nerve had been permanently affected by what happened earlier. But they continued without incident and reached the hut in the ruins of the monastery, to find it in darkness.

They stood for some moments looking out across the tops of the trees on the lower slopes. The bay was serenely peaceful. Moonlight glittered on its surface. The scene was beautiful, but Melissa shuddered as she recalled the fear that had assailed her on Gregory's boat.

Russell held her close. His presence was immensely reassuring. She looked up into his face and he slid his arms around her shoulders, drawing her into his embrace. She sighed and leaned her head against his shoulder, thankful that they had emerged safely from danger. Their mutual experience seemed to have drawn them even closer together. Russell must have been thinking the same thing, as he kissed her and held her close as if he would never let her go. But eventually he released her and held her arm to lead her back to the path.

'I dread to think how I would have ended up if you hadn't found me on Lombard's boat and rescued me,' he said. 'That took a lot of nerve, Melissa.'

'I didn't think so at the time; but looking back now, I'm wondering how I managed it,' she replied. 'It was really scary!'

'That's the understatement of the

month. I don't know how you feel right now, but I could do with a drink. If you'd like one too, we could go out to the yacht and indulge ourselves. I have to report to the professor anyway, and there are one or two loose ends that need tying up.'

'That sounds like a good idea. A nightcap might be just what a doctor would order.'

They walked down the path, which was now very familiar to Melissa, and gained the beach. The dinghy was drawn up out of the water. Moonlight shone on the smooth surface of the bay, and a solitary light was casting a dim gleam on the yacht. Russell helped Melissa into the dinghy and pushed off, then rowed strongly out to the yacht. The professor appeared on the deck as they reached the vessel, and held out a hand to Melissa when she stepped aboard.

'I've had a radio report on what happened earlier, Russell,' Professor Allen said, 'and I'm most unhappy at the way Melissa has been dragged into this affair.'

'I'd probably be dead by now if she hadn't stepped in to save me,' Russell replied.

'I'm most grateful for what she's done, but she mustn't be involved any further, even if it means you two not seeing each other after tonight. I'm very concerned about her safety.'

'We may not be in a position to see each other after this evening,' Russell countered. 'Melissa has been told her that services are no longer required at the villa.'

'I'm sorry to hear that.' The professor sighed and motioned for Melissa to sit down. 'Get some drinks, Russell,' he commanded, and Russell went below. 'I heard what Mrs Kemp did this morning,' he continued. 'If you hadn't acted so quickly, her suicide bid might have succeeded.'

'She was in little danger of drowning,' Melissa observed, 'and she seemed to be unaffected by her adventure. I don't think it was a serious suicide attempt; she did it to gain attention.'

'And why have your services been terminated?'

'I understand that Mrs Kemp is to be placed in a clinic or a nursing home.'

'That's most unsatisfactory. What will you do now?'

'I'll return to London, report to the bureau, and hopefully find another position.'

Russell appeared with a tray of bottles and glasses, and Melissa sat quietly, sipping white wine while the two men talked over recent events. She watched Russell, and felt saddened that her time on the island was going to end so soon and there appeared to be no future for them together. Were they fated to meet and part, never to see each other again? Russell had helped her to recover from the misery of her broken romance, but it seemed that they were not meant for each other, and she was desolate. And how would he continue after she departed? Would he miss her, or promptly forget about her and turn to Jasmine for solace? Melissa's thoughts turned sour and she moved restlessly.

She found Russell's gaze upon her. He was telling the professor what she had done to save him, and his face carried such an expression of thankfulness that she was overcome by emotion. She blinked rapidly as tears filled her eyes. She did not want to part from Russell. The knowledge stabbed through her mind and released a whole clutter of subconscious hopes and fears. The thought came to her that she was in love with him, and had been from the first moment she saw him.

'Are you ready to go back to the villa, Melissa?' Russell asked. 'You're looking very strained and tired. Finish your drink and I'll take you ashore. You need a good night's rest.'

She arose at once, thanked the professor for the drink, and walked to where the dinghy was moored. Russell jumped into the small boat and helped her down. She sat on the stern seat and Russell unshipped the oars. He sat facing her as he rowed strongly shoreward. The stars seemed brighter than she could ever remember seeing them before, and appreciation of their remote beauty uplifted her.

Tiny waves lapped against the bows of the dinghy as it moved slowly between the yacht and the shore, and the slight sounds they made seemed like the caresses of a benign mother nature smiling on their pleasure. Melissa drew a deep breath and then released it in a long sigh as she assimilated impressions of her surroundings that would remain with her for the rest of her life.

'This is too much like a dream,' she said, her voice echoing slightly in the surrounding silence. 'My life changed completely when I came here, and my hopes soared when I met you, but now it seems that everything is turning to ashes.'

'Life is like that,' Russell replied. 'But

don't give up hope, Melissa.'

She nodded, agreeing with what he said. But her hopes were at zero, for she was aware that there had been too much against them from the start. A troublesome situation had existed here before her arrival, and she had walked into it and become involved.

She was suddenly filled with trepidation as she thought of the previous evening, when Nick had reared up out of the sea and overturned the dinghy. But this evening was quiet and without incident. They soon reached the shore, where Russell beached the dinghy, and they walked up through the pines to the villa. He kissed Melissa goodnight and departed. She was exhausted as she went to her room.

Quickly she tumbled into bed, and knew nothing more until a rough hand on her shoulder jerked her awake. She opened her eyes to see Christopher Kemp standing over her.

11

'I've just heard that Gregory Lombard has been arrested,' Christopher rapped, 'and you were with Russell Vinson when it happened. I had doubts about you when I first saw you on the steamer. You were on the deck talking to Vinson as if you and he were old friends, and yet you were supposed to be strangers. So are you with the police? I doubt if you're a real nurse, the way you've been handling my mother.'

'How dare you come in here?' Melissa exclaimed. 'I know nothing about what's happening. Please leave my room.'

Christopher stared at her, his eyes narrowed, and he seemed to be trying to decide if she was telling the truth or not. Then he turned abruptly and departed, closing the bedroom door. Melissa breathed deeply to quell the fear assailing her. She slipped out of bed and went to the door, turned the key in the lock; and, aware that she was too deeply disturbed to sleep despite her tiredness, dressed and went down to the kitchen to make a hot drink.

As she sat down at the kitchen table, the front door slammed. Christopher was going out! She knew he was involved in the smuggling from what had happened when he had taken her out in his boat; and, fearing that he might be contemplating some action against Russell, she opened the back door, intending to check around the villa. When she heard feet crunching on the gravelled path at the side of the building, she switched off the light, closed the door, and turned the key silently in the lock.

She looked through the window, and a moment later saw Christopher hurrying along the path that led toward Gregory's chalet. Melissa shook her head, wondering what she should do, and a moment later a smaller figure appeared and hurried by. It was Gina! Melissa was shocked. She waited a moment before slipping out of the villa to follow her.

It was amazing how her tiredness vanished when concern for Russell arose in her mind. She hurried after Gina, determined to discover what was happening. Gina followed Christopher to the back of Gregory's chalet, and when Christopher saw police checking the chalet he dropped into cover and waited. Gina did likewise, and Melissa crouched behind a bush and watched them. But evidently Christopher was impatient, for after a few minutes he arose and went off to the right along a path that ran parallel to the shore and passed along the cliff in front of and below the Kemp villa.

Melissa followed when Gina moved in the same direction. Christopher reached a point on the path that was directly beneath the villa and turned left to descend a cliff path that was not obvious to the casual gaze. Gina waited a considerable time before following, and Melissa moved to the top of the concealed path and crouched, watching Gina descending to the beach. She reached the bottom and moved to the left, and Melissa hurried after her.

Gina disappeared into the dark mouth of a small cave in the cliff. Melissa paused when she got there. She was surprised to see the dim glow of an interior light well back inside. There was no sign of Christopher. She crouched to one side of the cave mouth to watch Gina, and stifled a gasp when Christopher suddenly rose up from the shadows and confronted her. Gina began shouting at him, evidently concerned about Nick. Christopher grasped her shoulders, quickly over-powered her struggles, and half-carried her deeper into the cave.

Melissa was shocked, unable to believe what she had seen. Then her concern for Gina galvanised her into action. She entered the cave and went forward. As she progressed, she saw the cave widen considerably; and when she rounded a slight bend, it broadened into a cavern that rose abruptly to a higher level, where she saw many bales and crates stacked against the walls. Marks on the lower wall showed that at high tide the lower cave was completely submerged.

Several electric lamps were fixed in the roof of the cavern, and by their ample light Melissa was able to see a flight of steps at the end of the cave that led up to a solid wooden door. There was no sign of Christopher or Gina, and she assumed that they had passed into an inner chamber. Afraid for Gina's safety, Melissa ascended the steps and tried the door, which opened readily. She entered a tunnel that sloped upwards rather steeply to the right. Electric lights were attached at intervals to the ceiling.

Melissa was relieved, but she was deeply concerned for Gina. She looked around. There was a door on the left-hand side of the tunnel similar to the one she had passed through. A key was in a lock on the door. She turned it, pulled the door open, and saw Gina huddled inside a chamber that was shelved to contain many small packages and larger containers, all evidently contraband.

Gina did not move as Melissa approached her. She was unconscious, her left temple swollen. Melissa lifted her into a more comfortable position and called her name. At first there was no reply, and Melissa gently shook her shoulder while repeatedly calling her name. Eventually Gina opened her eyes and gazed up at Melissa. She was frightened, and looked around quickly.

'Where's Christopher?' she demanded.

'He's gone, so don't worry.'

'But he'll be back,' Gina gasped. 'He said he'd return at high tide, when the outer cave is filled with water, and then he was going to drown me!'

'I don't think even Christopher would go that far,' Melissa observed.

'He's gone further. Nick told me

Christopher killed his brother Kenneth seven years ago because he found out about the smuggling.'

Melissa stared aghast at the trembling woman, her mind reeling in shock at the revelation. She shook her head, unable to accept the grim fact. Gina saw her reaction and grasped her hands. 'It's true,' she said fearfully. 'Nick found out about it, and that's why he can't break away from the smugglers. Christopher would kill him without hesitation.'

'How long have you known about Kenneth Kemp's murder?' Melissa asked.

'Nick heard Christopher talking about it to Gregory one night. Gregory was reluctant to go along with Christopher's plans to expand the smuggling business, but Christopher threatened him with the exposure of his part in Kenneth's murder. Kenneth had found out about Christopher's smuggling, and gave him a week to finish with the business. But Christopher had no intention of stopping, and when Kenneth went sailing one night, Gregory took Christopher out to Kenneth's boat and waited while Christopher went aboard, killed his brother, tied an anchor to the body and pushed it overboard.'

'So that's why Kenneth's body was never found,' Melissa muttered. 'We'd better get out of here, Gina. If Christopher catches us, we wouldn't have a chance against him. Come on, we'll go back to the outer tunnel and escape that way. The sooner we tell Russell about this, the better. Are you all right to move?'

'It'll be useless to run. Christopher will come after me as soon as he finds I've got out,' Gina protested.

'Russell will protect you,' Melissa insisted.

They returned to the lower tunnel and made their way to the exit. Melissa held Gina's hand and helped her along, and they finally stumbled out to the beach to find the tide coming in swiftly.

Gripping Gina's hand, Melissa set off at a run along the beach to the path that led up to Gregory's chalet, impatient to contact the police who were still searching it.

They traversed the path and ascended quickly. When they reached the top, a uniformed Greek policeman stepped out of the shadows and accosted them.

'Tell him we're looking for Russell Vinson,' Melissa prompted Gina, who spoke quickly in Greek.

'Ah! You are the English lady we were told about,' the policeman said in English, addressing Melissa. 'I am sorry, but Inspector Vinson is not here. He and his associate went into town to check the boat the smugglers have been using.'

'Can you contact him please?' Melissa asked. 'We need to give him some important information as soon as possible.'

'Come with me,' the policeman said. 'I have a radio in my car, and I can call the car that is taking the Englishmen to town.'

Melissa sighed with relief as they accompanied him. They passed around the chalet to a police car on the back road. The policeman used his radio, and Melissa waited in a flood of anxiety, wanting Christopher to be arrested before he could add to his crimes. Finally, the policeman finished his call and turned to Melissa.

'The two English policemen are on their way back here,' he said.

'You'd better stay here, Gina,' Melissa said without hesitation. 'Tell Russell everything you know. I'll get back to the villa and check on Mrs Kemp.'

'But if Christopher sees you, he might harm you,' Gina gasped.

'He doesn't suspect me of anything. I can come and go as I please. At the moment you're the one in danger.'

'Please be careful,' Gina begged.

Melissa waited until Gina went into the chalet, accompanied by the policeman, before turning to return to the villa. She entered through the kitchen and went up to Mrs Kemp's room to check on her patient. To her relief, Mrs Kemp was still sleeping peacefully. She watched the relaxed face of her patient, and shook her head sadly as she imagined the horror that would descend on the woman if she learned that one of her sons had killed the other.

She locked the door of the room and went to her own room, and knew even as she switched on the light that she had made a bad error of judgement, for Christopher was standing behind the door. He slammed it as soon she entered the room, grasped her shoulder roughly, forced her across to the bed, and threw her down upon it. She looked up at him, filled with shock. The expression on his face warned her that she had badly underestimated him.

'You've been taking me for a fool!' he said angrily. 'You were acting the innocent nurse, while all along you've been working secretly with Russell Vinson, spying on me.'

'I have no idea what you're talking about,' Melissa gasped. 'Where do you get such crazy ideas?'

'I've had a telephone call from Gregory Lombard. He told me you were on his boat this evening with Vinson. You sneaked aboard and freed him, and he stole the boat and brought it back to the harbour. A customs boat went out after Gregory, but he got clear. It seems that I have you to thank for this situation. Now I have to get out in a hurry, and I'm taking you with me as a hostage. I'll steal Vinson's yacht and rendezvous with Gregory out in the strait. We'll go to Albania until this blows over.'

'You can't take me away from here,' Melissa protested. 'There's no one in the house to care for your mother. If she wakes and no one attends her, anything could happen.'

'I've telephoned Andrea. She's on her way back from town and will get here in a few minutes. So come along. You're going for another boat trip with me, and this time it'll be on a one-way ticket.'

He dragged Melissa up from the bed and forced her to the door. She struggled, but he was too strong for her and she was forced to accompany him out of the villa and down the path to the beach. Russell's dinghy lay just above the water's edge, and out in the bay the professor's yacht was ghostly white in the moonlight.

Melissa was really afraid. Christopher had killed his brother to seal his lips, and she had no doubt that he would carry out his threat to deal with her in the same callous manner.

12

Christopher grasped Melissa's arm and pushed her towards the dinghy, but the next instant he thrust her to the ground, dropped beside her and pressed a hand over her mouth to prevent an outcry. Melissa looked around and saw a small boat being rowed toward the beach. A larger vessel was moored beside the professor's yacht. Christopher removed his hand from her mouth.

'That's Gregory coming,' he said. 'We have to clear out of here now, thanks to your meddling, and we'll have to shift our stock.'

The bow of the incoming dinghy grated on the sand, and Gregory stepped from it. He stared at Melissa but said nothing. Christopher pushed Melissa forward, holding her left elbow.

'There's been a lot of trouble this evening,' said he sharply. 'Everything's gone wrong, and it's all down to you, Gregory. You've been getting lax lately, and letting Melissa sneak aboard your boat to turn Vinson loose was the height of carelessness. I'm lucky to still be free, and we might have trouble getting away. I'm hoping we can load our supplies on that boat out there. Our two boats are in the harbour, swarming with police.'

'Forget about the merchandise.' Gregory's tone was filled with panic. 'The tide isn't high enough to get a boat into the cave, and we can't wait around for another two hours. Leave with me now, or stay and face arrest.'

'We've got a fortune tied up in that contraband. I'm not running empty-handed,' Christopher protested. 'Hold on to your nerve.'

'We can't salvage anything! If you try, you'll get caught. We must save ourselves, and time's running out. Come away now. I'm not waiting any longer. The Albanians didn't want to come this far, so get a move on. What are you going to do with Melissa? We can't leave her here. She knows too much.'

'She's the least of our worries. We'll take her along, and drop her overboard when we get into the strait.'

Melissa shivered at Christopher's cold tone.

'I'll have nothing to do with harming her,' Gregory protested.

'You took Vinson out in your boat to get rid of him.'

'That was different. He had to be dealt with, and I intended to pass him over to the Albanians to do it. Turn her loose now and come with me. We don't have much time.'

'I'm not leaving without the goods, and you'll bring your dinghy to the cave. The tide should be high enough now to float a couple of small boats. We'll load them and then pull out. I'll put Melissa in the strong room in the cave. I've got Gina in there already. She was following me earlier. She's gone over the top about Nick.'

'I could slip along to my chalet and collect some personal items,' Gregory said.

'I wouldn't if I were you.' Christopher laughed harshly. 'The police are there in force.'

Gregory muttered under his breath, and Melissa experienced a pang of hope. If she was locked in the room where Gina had been held, then she would have a chance of being discovered by the police when they searched the villa. She did not protest when Christopher pushed her into the dinghy and began rowing to the left, a few yards clear of the shore.

Gregory followed in his boat, and when they were directly in line with the villa on the cliff, Melissa was surprised to see that the tide was flooding into the cave mouth. The dinghy was swept into the total darkness of the cave by the inrushing tide and carried up against the side of the shelf at the rear.

'Don't try to get away in here,' Christopher warned. 'Stay quiet and I'll leave you here, but give me trouble and I'll take you out into the strait and toss you overboard.'

Melissa did not reply. Eventually the bow of the dinghy struck rock, and Christopher jumped out into the darkness. There were several moments of silence and inactivity, and then overhead lights flashed on. The incoming tide was creeping higher up the rock wall, as if intent on flooding the higher level of the cavern.

Christopher stood above the dinghy. 'Come on up,' he commanded.

Melissa obeyed. When she gained the upper level, she looked down and saw Gregory bringing his boat alongside.

'Start loading your dinghy,' Christopher shouted at him. 'I'm going to lock Melissa in the storeroom.' He grasped her arm and propelled her toward the flight of steps that led up to the door at the rear of the cave. When they got there, he pushed her ahead to precede him, and then followed her. When they were about twenty steps up to the door, Melissa realised that if she was going to do something about escaping, then the most opportune moment had arrived.

She reached the top step and paused. Christopher reached past her to grasp the handle of the door, and it then that she half-turned towards him, placed her hands on his shoulders, and pushed against him with all her strength.

Christopher uttered a yell of surprise and went over backwards. He grasped at Melissa as he lost balance, but his clawing fingers missed her by a hair's breadth. She watched him fall all the way down the steps to the bottom. His head struck the rock floor and he subsided into an inert heap.

Gregory came running. Melissa turned to the door, pulled it open, and passed through to the upper tunnel. She slammed the door and started running along the right-hand tunnel, with no idea where it would lead her, but flight was the only possibility. She heard the door behind her crash open, and Gregory's voice echoed unintelligibly at her back. When she risked a glance over her shoulder, she saw him pursuing her, and redoubled her efforts.

Gregory gained on her, and Melissa began to despair. He called to her, ordering her to stop, but she continued, gazing ahead hopefully until she saw a blank wall confronting her, with steps to one side leading up to what looked like a trapdoor overhead. But she realised that Gregory was too close behind her now: he would reach her before she could negotiate the steps. Even as the thought crossed her mind, his powerful hands closed on her shoulders from behind and pulled her to a halt.

'There's no need for this stupidity,' he gasped, his shoulders heaving. 'I'll lock you in the chamber, and you'll be safe in there until the police arrive. Come along, and don't give me any trouble. All I want to do is get away from here.'

He began to lead her back along the tunnel, holding her left arm. Melissa was exhausted; there was no more resistance left in her. She allowed herself to be taken, and they were close to the door that led into the cavern when it was suddenly thrust open. Melissa gasped in shock as a figure appeared in the doorway. She expected it to be Christopher, but the familiar figure of Russell came forward, followed closely by three uniformed Greek policemen.

Gregory reacted swiftly. He turned and started running back along the tunnel to the steps at the far end.

'You can't get away, Lombard!' Russell shouted. 'We've got men entering from the cellar in the villa, and they'll be here in a moment. You're cut off.'

Melissa gazed at Russell in wonder. He looked at her and his grim expression faded. He smiled and came to her. She collapsed into his arms and he held her close. His lips brushed her forehead as her knees weakened.

'Gina told us about this place,' he said, looking down into her pale face. 'We've got Christopher in the cavern. He'd had a fall before we arrived, and his right leg is broken.'

'Let me go to him,' Melissa said instantly. 'Perhaps I can help him until you can get proper medical help.'

'An ambulance is on its way from town. There's nothing you can do for him. A policeman is with him. Come with me and I'll take you up into the villa. Gina's up there now.'

He led her back up the tunnel. Gregory was ahead of them, negotiating the steps at the far end. Just as he reached the trapdoor over his head, it was jerked open, and several policemen came hurriedly down the steps. Gregory turned to run back again, then saw Russell and several policemen advancing on him from below. He halted and raised his hands. He was surrounded by policemen and taken up into the villa.

Russell escorted Melissa up the steps,

through the trapdoor, and into a cellar. They ascended another flight of steps and emerged in the villa, in a passage that led to the kitchen.

'Are you all right, Melissa?' Russell asked.

'They didn't harm me,' she replied, and began shaking uncontrollably.

'You need a strong drink.' He led her into the library. Andrea was seated at the desk, and arose when she saw Melissa.

'I'm sorry you've been subjected to such an ordeal,' she said. 'I had no idea what was going on here, and when Christopher telephoned me earlier to say you were leaving I rushed over. What made you decide to go so abruptly?'

'It was Christopher's decision,' Melissa replied. 'He said your father called from the mainland to say your mother was to go back into a clinic, so my services were no longer required.'

'Well that's not true. I hope you'll stay on to take care of my mother. I thought you were doing extremely well with her. I've spoken to my father on the telephone and he's coming back from the mainland tomorrow. He said he'll talk to you then.'

Melissa nodded. Russell came to her with a glass of brandy, and her teeth clicked against the rim of the glass as she drank some of its contents. Russell stayed at her side, watching her intently. She met his gaze and he smiled encouragingly. She told him about the boat tied up against the professor's yacht, and he nodded.

'We've been watching it for some time,' he said. 'The police could have arrested its crew just after we escaped with Lombard's boat, but they held off because it was thought they would try to salvage their stock and we might catch them in the act.'

Melissa sat down on a chair and tried to relax. Her thoughts were haphazard and unsettled, and she watched Russell, waiting for her mind to stop whirling and become calm again. Was this terrifying adventure finally at an end?

Russell took the glass from her hand. 'Come with me for a walk. My part in this is finished now until the trials take place. Nick's given us a great deal of information, and the local police are acting on it. I expect you'll be called later as a witness, but apart from that it's all over.'

Melissa stood up rather unsteadily. Russell tucked his hand under her arm and led her to the door, which opened as they reached it. Jasmine appeared, and she halted when she saw them.

'So you've got Melissa, sir,' she said crisply. 'I've been looking around the outhouses and sheds for her. Are you all right, Melissa?'

Melissa gazed at her. Jasmine saw the expression of shock on Melissa's face and grinned. 'So you didn't tell her that I'm a policewoman, Inspector?'

'I couldn't,' Russell said. 'I wanted her to believe that I was seeing you because we were supposed to be having an affair.'

'How could you, sir? What would my husband say if he knew you played fast and loose with my reputation?' Jasmine grinned at Melissa. 'I'm a happily married woman!'

Russell smiled at Melissa. 'I knew you'd followed me up to the monastery and watched me go into the hut, but I couldn't explain the situation. In fact, I was visiting Detective Sergeant Jasmine Pollard to get her daily report, which I've done every night while we've been on the island.'

Melissa felt her doubts drain away. Russell saw her expression change. He grasped her arm. 'I still have my security round to do,' he said, smiling, 'and I've become so used to your company, I'd like you to come along with me.'

Melissa nodded, although she could feel a strange weakness seeping into her. She leaned heavily against Russell, and he looked down at her with grave concern in his expression.

'You look as if you could do with

some fresh air,' he said. 'I know I could. We had rather a testing time together on Lombard's boat. I don't know how to thank you for what you've done. Words don't seem to be enough. It's strange, but your arrival triggered a series of events that helped our investigation immensely, and we're deeply indebted to you.'

Melissa sagged, and would have fallen if Russell had not caught her in his strong arms and swept her up off her feet. She could feel his heart pounding against her breast, and closed her eyes as he lowered his head and took possession of her lips. She squirmed in his arms as his kiss deepened and drew a natural response from her. He carried her outside into the open air and she relaxed for the first time in hours.

Suddenly her heart was singing. A scented breeze was coming across the terrace, bringing something of the island's magic in its breath, and everything slipped back into its normal perspective.

'It might be possible that we'll be

able to spend some time together now.' Russell set her feet on the terrace and supported her, but she straightened, already feeling stronger.

'What a good idea!' she said. 'I'd like that very much. Now let's take that walk.'

They went to the path that led up to the monastery and walked along it with resolute steps, as if it were a highway leading into the future. Melissa glanced up at Russell and opened her mouth to speak as he put his arms around her, then realised that the time for words was past.

Russell's lips taking possession of her mouth was all that mattered. Whatever else came up in future, she would never forget this wonderful island or the circumstances that had led her to meeting this wonderful man. She clung to him as if afraid she was dreaming — and then thought that if this was just a dream, she never wanted to awaken.

We do hope that you have enjoyed reading this large print book.

Did you know that all of our titles are available for purchase?

We publish a wide range of high quality large print books including:
Romances, Mysteries, Classics
General Fiction
Non Fiction and Westerns

Special interest titles available in large print are:
The Little Oxford Dictionary
Music Book, Song Book
Hymn Book, Service Book

Also available from us courtesy of Oxford University Press:
Young Readers' Dictionary
(large print edition)
Young Readers' Thesaurus
(large print edition)

For further information or a free brochure, please contact us at:
Ulverscroft Large Print Books Ltd.,
The Green, Bradgate Road, Anstey,
Leicester, LE7 7FU, England.
Tel: (00 44) **0116 236 4325**
Fax: (00 44) **0116 234 0205**

IN PERFECT HARMONY

Wendy Kremer

When Holly Watson starts work as a PA to music director Ian Travers, she's hoping for a simple part-time job to earn a little extra. She gets more than she bargained for, however — her new boss stirs decidedly unprofessional feelings within her. But she's not the only one so affected: Olivia de Noiret, a beautiful and sophisticated prima donna soprano, also has her eyes on Ian — and makes it very clear to Holly that she's already staked her claim . . .

CHRISTMAS IN THE BAY

Jo Bartlett

Maddie Jones runs a bookshop in the beautiful St Nicholas Bay. Devoted to her business, she's forgotten what it's like to have a romantic life — until Ben Cartwright arrives, and reminds her of what she's missing. But Ben isn't being entirely honest about what brings him to town — and when his professional ambition threatens Maddie's livelihood, their relationship seems doomed. When a flash flood descends on the Bay, all the community must pull together — will Ben stay or go?

NOTHING BUT THE BEST

Margaret Sutherland

Natalie's boyfriend Philip is a high-powered, successful surgeon. But while she feels safe and secure in his arms, she resents the way he bottles up his feelings; and how can she challenge him about the long hours he works, when he's doing it to save lives? When Philip discovers that he has inherited a dilapidated seaside cottage from his estranged father, and Natalie must undergo a serious operation, both of them are forced to examine their relationship and decide whether it's likely to stand the test of time.